Philomena *(Unloved)*

Philomena *(Unloved)*

a novel by

Christene A. Browne

Second Story Press
www.secondstorypress.ca

Library and Archives Canada Cataloguing in Publication

Browne, Christene, author
Philomena (unloved) / a novel by Christene A. Browne.
Issued in print and electronic formats.

ISBN 978-1-77260-076-6 (softcover).--ISBN 978-1-77260-077-3 (HTML)
I. Title.
PS8603.R697P45 2018   C813'.6   C2018-902788-6
C2018-902789-4

Copyright © 2018 by Christene A. Browne

Printed and bound in Canada
Text © Christene A. Browne
Cover image © Talya Baldwin, i2iart.com
Edited by Kathy White
Designed by Ellie Sipila

Second Story Press gratefully acknowledges the support of the Ontario Arts Council and the Canada Council for the Arts for our publishing program. We acknowledge the financial support of the Government of Canada through the Canada Book Fund.

Published by
SECOND STORY PRESS
20 Maud Street, Suite 401
Toronto, ON M5V 2M5
www.secondstorypress.ca

To the one in three
who have fallen victim to sexual violence
and one in five
who suffer from mental illness.

Chapter 1

Philomena *ph(i)-lome-na, phil(o)-mena* \ *as a girl's name is of Greek origin, meaning "powerful love."*

WHEN MY MOTHER left, I had just turned two and was still in the process of discovering my voice. It was small and didn't have very many words, but I made an effort to use it to speak to her each night. By the time I was four, I was able to hold meaningful conversations.

Each evening, after I had said my prayers, I would brush the dust from my knees, get in bed, and whisper to her as if she were there.

"How you doing today?" I'd ask. "I hope that you're keeping nice and warm. I hear that the place where you live now is cold, even colder than Mrs. Gumb's icebox."

My mother's replies were often rushed or hurried. I blamed it on the weather. On the island, people always rushed and were in foul moods when it rained. I assumed that people would be even more irritated in the cold.

I went to sleep every day with the memory of my mother's warmth. It comforted me when I was lonely and cloaked me in goodness when I needed some assurance that life was not all bad.

Philomena (Unloved)

When I was five, I decided to write to her. I asked my teacher for help with the spelling since she was more patient than my grandmother.

After the words were learned, I carefully ripped out the last piece of paper in my notebook, sat on the floor in the corner of the front room, and printed in my best handwriting. My work was neat since my grandmother had made me practice my letters since I was three.

"I don't want you writing any chicken scratch," she would say.

The first letter wasn't long. I didn't know what to say.

> *Dear Mother,*
> *I love you. I hope to see you again soon.*
> *Love,*
> *Philomena*

I folded the paper, searched the trunk where my grandmother kept all of the important things, found a brand-new blue-and-white airmail envelope, and slipped my letter inside.

"Can you please send this for me?" I asked my grandmother, hoping that I wouldn't be punished for *going into places I had no business going into.*

"What's this?" She yanked the envelope out of my hand. "Who told you to touch up my things? What is it? A letter? Who you writing to in my good envelope?"

"My mother."

"Your mother?" She looked at me sideways, the same way she looked at people when she suspected that they were lying or cheating.

"Yes," I said firmly, trying to quell whatever misgivings she might have had.

"Who put that idea in your head?"

"Me."

"Who showed you how to write so good?"
"You."
A flash of a smile lit up her normally sour face.
"So, what did you write to your mother?" She removed the letter from the envelope.
"Hmm," she said. "You spelled everything good. Who showed you?"
"My teacher."
"Hmm. So, you want me to post it?"
"Yes, please."
"You shouldn't get your hopes up, though. You know how many letters I sent her and didn't get an answer? Too many to count."
"It doesn't matter, I just want to send it."
"Okay, I'll put it with my next letter."
I was so happy, I almost hugged her.

As my writing skills improved, I wrote longer, more detailed letters. I told my mother about my lessons at school, the weather, the neighbor's quarrels, or whatever else I could think of. There were certain things, however, I knew never to mention.

It took almost two years before I received a blue-and-white airmail envelope that was addressed to me. Before that, my mother had just sent her greetings via the odd letter she wrote to my grandmother. I liked to think it was my letters that got her writing again.

I laughed out loud when the envelope with my name spelled out in capital letters, followed by our address, St. Peter's, Montserrat, W. I., was placed in my hand. It looked as if great care had been taken to write it.

"For me?" I said in the loudest and happiest voice I had ever heard myself use.

My grandmother gave me such a look that I thought she would swat me, but she just left me alone.

I sat down on my bed and ripped the envelope open. I was careful not to tear the part with my name.

Dear Philomena,

How are you keeping, my child? Thank you so much for your letters. Your handwriting is getting better all the time. I hope that you are being a good girl for your grandmother.

The weather here is very hot now, even hotter than back home if you could believe it. Sorry I have not been able to send for you yet. Things are very difficult here. I hope this letter finds you well.

Love,

Your mother

The words *Your mother* stood out like a shiny beacon on the page. I touched and kissed the words as if they were my mother herself. Their existence in front of me proved that she was real, that she did exist, and that she was not just a figment of my imagination. She was as real as the paper, the ink, the envelope, and the hand that was holding it. As I peered down at the writing, which was not at all chicken scratch, I imagined what she looked like. I had forgotten her face since there wasn't a single picture to remind me. I caressed the word *mother*, and there she was standing right in front of me. She wore a beautiful yellow summer dress with narrow straps that hugged her thin shoulders. On her head was a large-brimmed straw hat that made her look more glamorous and beautiful than anyone I had ever seen. Her bare feet shuffled over the hot sand. When I waved at her, she wiggled her fingers at me, then took off her hat and began fanning her face and neck.

"This blasted heat is too much for me," she complained.

"Why don't you drink some water," I suggested.

"I would prefer some limeade," she replied, putting the hat back on her head.

"Would you like me to make some for you?" I offered.

"Sure," she said. "Just wait one minute." She turned around and vanished.

"Wait, you forgot the limeade. I haven't made it yet. Please come back, please."

I pleaded with her for a short while and then gave up. I don't think my grandmother heard me, either that or she pretended not to. Our beds were in the same room not far from each other. I suspected that there may have been something wrong with her hearing. She never heard anyone when people called out to her in the road. It was either her failing ears or her intolerance for *bad manners*. I never knew.

Each time my mother wrote, I would imagine her in whatever condition she described. She once told me about having to go to the hospital. I imagined her with bandages from head to toe lying stiff in a sterile room.

"Can I get anything for you, a glass of water, something to read?" I asked her.

I tried not to show her how scared I was.

"I'm fine, but could you fix my pillow?"

I did as she asked. "Would you like to relax now?" I felt guilty about disturbing her sleep. I knew that sick people needed their rest.

The letters continued until I was ten. Then they stopped. Those to my grandmother also stopped. This didn't surprise her at all.

"It's a miracle she kept sending them for so long. I know just how selfish and inconsiderate that girl can be."

I didn't agree. I believed in my mother. I had faith that the letters would return. I knew she thought of me often since I was her only child. I believed that she could never truly abandon me. However, when the letters didn't resume after six months, then a year, and for some time after that, I marked my grandmother's words. Outwardly, however, I expressed otherwise.

"Maybe she's sick again and that's why she can't write anymore."

"Sick people can get others to write for them," my grandmother insisted.

"Maybe she lost her hands or her eyes in an accident," I said in my mother's defense.

"Even blind people with no hands can still get other people to write letters for them." I knew my grandmother was right. There was no excuse.

Chapter 2

THEY LEFT ME naked in the room. The bandage on my head was my only covering. They said I was a risk to myself. *What harm could someone do with underwear*, I wondered? Maybe they thought I would stuff it into my mouth and choke or strangle myself with the elastic. There weren't even sheets on the bed. What good were sheets if there were no windows in the padded room? I spent the first hours pacing, trying to piece through the events that had brought me to that place. Not just the recent ones, but everything in the past. My thoughts were a jumbled mess. Fatigued, I took a seat in the corner, the same way I had done when I was child. The cold cement, however, was not as hospitable as my grandmother's wooden floor. After only a few minutes, it became unbearable. The plastic mattress was the only other option. I didn't like the way it clung to my skin. Sleep didn't come easy.

The next day, I found myself in a regular hospital room, surrounded by sterile gauze and shiny surfaces, not even sure how I had gotten there. The bandage was still in place. Someone had the decency to put a hospital gown on me. An IV drip had also been attached to my arm. I didn't remember them putting that in either.

Philomena (Unloved)

A draft wafted from the window. Outside was miserable. Not a sliver of sunshine in the sky, no blue either. As I strained my head upward to see if I could recognize any buildings, I felt a tap on my shoulder. It was a nurse dressed in orange scrubs that made her look like a prisoner. She forced a smile and checked my IV without saying a word. On her way out she glanced quickly at the bed next to the door. I hadn't realized that I had company.

My neighbor was so still, I suspected that she might have been in a coma. I couldn't see her face so there was no way of knowing who she was or what she looked like. I kept my eyes glued to her torso to make sure she was still alive. The up and down movement of the blue blanket comforted me for some reason. It reminded me of waves. I fell asleep watching it.

When I awoke, a man with large arms was hovering over me. He looked as if he had eaten a whole cow for breakfast. His biceps were so muscular and shiny, they appeared to be plastic. They called out to be touched, but I didn't dare.

"I have to take you for your treatment." He spoke slowly, pronouncing every word carefully. "Do you understand me?"

My reply was a confused stare. I had no idea what he was talking about. I glanced quickly at my motionless neighbor and then the window. Neither offered any explanation.

"I'm supposed to take you to see Doctor Rueben. I am going to lift you up now," he continued.

There was a wheelchair already waiting next to my bed. I stared at the top of his balding head as he settled me into the chair. "Okay, ready to roll," he said as he stepped behind me. I could feel his breath sitting heavy on my skull. It made me uncomfortable.

"Let's get out of here." I tried to get a better look at my roommate as we rolled by, but we were moving too fast.

The treatment room was on the fifth floor. It was dark and cold inside. The orderly transferred me onto the examining table and then trodded away. I tried to make myself comfortable as the stiff disposable paper of the examining table bunched up beneath me. I stopped when I noticed I had an audience. The doctor, a tall, pale man, and two young students, one male and one female, stood staring at me quietly from the other side of the room.

They huddled together and whispered. Their voices were as incoherent as the bleating of sheep.

"This is her first treatment, so it shouldn't be too aggressive."

"How many more will she need?"

"That will depend on how she responds this time."

The doctor stepped toward me with his hands shoved deep into the pockets of his lab coat. If I didn't know better, I would have sworn he was fishing for his penis.

"How're you doing there, Miss Jones? My name is Doctor Rueben. I saw you last week when you came in."

I had no recollection of seeing him.

"As we discussed, we are going to be starting your treatment today. It shouldn't be too taxing, but you may feel a little tired afterward."

The discussion that he referred to had also slipped my mind.

"If you have any questions or if you, at any time, feel any discomfort, please let us know."

The doctor looked at the students and nodded. The female student stuck some round silver things to either side of my head and chest while the doctor injected something into the IV drip. I had a million questions, but I didn't ask one. Instead, I turned my head to the floor and stared at their shadows on the linoleum as they fussed over me. Their blurred outlines seemed much more real.

The male student touched my forearm and handed me a Dixie Cup filled with water. It was as warm as piss. With his salty fingers, he slipped a pill into my mouth. I swallowed it in one quick gulp. Then he passed me a rubber mouth guard that looked as if it should have been thrown out long ago.

"What am I supposed to do with this?" I finally asked indignantly.

The student looked at the doctor.

"It's perfectly fine, Miss Jones. We use it so that the patients don't bite their tongues or injure their teeth."

His explanation did nothing to quell my fears. My thoughts shifted from worrying about the cleanliness of the mouth guard to the procedure itself. *What exactly are they doing to me?*

Leaving me naked in the padded room was bad enough, but now the overused mouth guard! "Is it necessary?" I asked.

"Like I said, it will prevent you from biting . . ."

"I mean the treatment."

"Yes, yes, of course it's necessary. Like we discussed, this treatment has proven to be very effective in cases like yours."

Again, I had no idea what he was talking about. All I knew was that I was beginning to feel listless and light-headed. Tiny droplets of drool started to pool at the corners of my mouth. I didn't have the energy to offer any more objections or ask any more questions. I attributed my lethargy to whatever had been injected into the IV. It was now in full effect. The male student put the mouth guard in place.

"Okay, so, if you don't have any more questions, I think we will just go ahead."

The doctor took a step toward a small white box on the shelf against the wall, gazed down at me, and nodded.

"Everything all right there?"

I didn't have the energy to move my head or open my mouth.

"Yes? Okay then," he continued.

He reached over and pressed a large red button on the box.

There was a word written on it, but I couldn't make it out. The female student appeared nervous as she observed the readout from another box. The male student clung close to my side. He smelled of salami and Irish Spring. While they waited for God knows what, they stared at me as if I had six arms and four legs. When nothing happened, they looked at each other confused.

I shifted my eyes to a brown leak spot on the ceiling as if nothing that they were doing had anything to do with me.

"Oops, I don't think I pushed hard enough. Let's try this again." The doctor chuckled as he made a second attempt.

I felt the results immediately. My body became stiff, then I began to twist and convulse. The spasms lasted only a minute but were intense. My eyes remained fixed on the brown spot on the ceiling. I shook and twitched one last time, then felt myself drift off. I sensed bodies moving around me as I slept.

A dull pulsing sensation ran through both of my legs and my lower jaw when I awoke. Not remembering where I was, my eyes darted around the room. I was startled by what appeared to be a disembodied head swimming toward me. It was gone when I blinked. I felt for my mouth. My tongue and teeth were still there. The mouth guard was gone.

"How you doing there? It's all over now, but you should rest a little longer," said Mr. Irish Spring in his best bedside manner. The doctor and the female student were no longer there.

I rolled on my side, closed my eyes, and fell back asleep. I felt the glare of Mr. Irish Spring's eyes on me all the while.

Chapter 3

MY GRANDMOTHER, PHILOMENA Ratina Jones, was a robust, woman with high cheekbones and a broad face. She prided herself on being a good Christian—but good didn't necessarily mean agreeable. I found this out when I was brought to live with her. One look at her sour face and I knew I had arrived in a den of inhospitality.

Ratina, as everyone called her, had raised eight children and six grandchildren. By the time I was delivered to her doorstep, most of the children and grandchildren were grown and had left the island. My mother, her youngest child, had been living with the family of my dead father. She didn't like them very much but stayed because they had a nice house with an indoor toilet. They didn't care much for her either since they believed she was responsible for my father's death. This is what I was told by my grandmother. I knew nothing about it, or my father for that matter, since he had died months before I was born. I had no recollection, either, of the day my mother left. I could only piece together what had transpired from my grandmother's grumblings. The rest I imagined. I would often replay the fictionalized scenario in my head.

"I don't understand why you can't just take the child with you," Ratina said. "I'm not fit for this anymore. Can't you see that?"

"I told you, Ma. It'll be easier if I go without her. I can find work and make things better for both of us," my mother responded as she wiped some sweat from her upper lip. She was roasting in the wool sweater she wore in preparation for her flight.

"And what about her father's family?" my grandmother asked.

"I can't leave my child with that pack of mongooses!"

"You're calling your dead husband's family mongooses?"

"Yes, that's what they are."

"So, what am I supposed to do with her and what about my peace?"

"You'll have plenty of that when I send for her, I promise, Ma. It's not going to be long. I'll send money and clothes, whatever she needs."

"That's not the problem."

"Then what is it?"

"I don't know if I'm able."

"Of course you are. And you'll see, she won't be any bother at all. She's a little angel."

"Angel or not, that's not the point."

"Ma, we've had this discussion a million times already. I don't know why you're bringing it up again. The taxi is waiting for me. I have to go," my mother said. She kissed me tenderly on the forehead and passed me over to Ratina's unwelcoming arms.

The lingering warmth of my mother's lips was the only real memory I had of that day.

Afterward, whenever I cried for my mother, Ratina would always stamp her feet and say, "You want to cry child, then cry all you like. Crying is not going to change a damn thing."

As time went on, I cried less, while Ratina did everything

to show me just how tired of minding children she was. Her calloused palms scratched me when she bathed me. Her wrist tugged harder than necessary when she combed my hair. She spoke in gruff tones, and when she cooked, the food was often burnt.

"I know it tastes like the soles of a shoe, but it's all we have," she would announce each time she placed a plate in front of me.

Accustomed to being fed by my mother, I had to learn to feed myself. I did so without a whimper because I knew that any shade of disobedience would not be tolerated.

Eventually I adapted to Ratina's cold distance. I said very little and did nothing that would upset her. At the age of four, my days were spent idling in the field that surrounded our three-room house. In the lush greenness, I spoke to myself and my mother while I snacked on the overripe mangoes and guavas that had fallen to the ground. I made sure to get all of my chats out of the way so it was easier to remain still and quiet indoors.

"What a lovely day. Yes, yes, it is. We haven't had any rain in days. But it's much better when it rains. It's better for the trees. Oh, the trees look just fine. Look at all those mangoes pulling them down." I would go on and on trying not to forget the sound of my voice.

In the evenings, before my prayers and my private conversations with my mother, I played with the toys that had been left behind by my cousins in the room that I shared with Ratina. The only toy that I could call my own was a wooden top I had found in the field. I made sure to keep it hidden from Ratina. Had she seen the dirty thing, she would have flung it back where it came from and pinched my arm for good measure. "Decent children don't play with garbage," she would have said.

Ratina didn't have very many friends. The only people who visited with any regularity were her customers. The ones from the church were the most loyal. So convinced of her clairvoyance, these people emptied their pockets just to hear their fortunes. They followed her instructions and always came under the cover of night, knocked three times, and whispered, "I've come to seek my destiny."

After the payments were deposited, which could be any combination of money, food, or fabric, they would ask their question before taking a seat in our tiny sitting room.

"Will my husband ever come back from Cuba?" Mrs. Payne, a wiry woman, asked one night.

Before answering, Ratina looked at the offering. She knew from experience that generosity usually meant desperation. When she saw that Mrs. Payne had not only brought some of her homemade bread and preserves but had also left several bills next to them, she was pleased.

"No, he's not coming back," Ratina replied. Like everyone else she had heard that Mr. Payne had met a young woman in Cuba.

"Will I ever hear from him?"

"No, he's finished with his life here."

"Will he ever send any money to help look after his children?"

Ratina rubbed her temples, closed her eyes, and pretended to slip into deep concentration.

"You may get something after he dies but not before," she replied, with her eyes still fully shut.

After Mrs. Payne was satisfied, she walked to the door, looked down, turned around, and exited backward.

Ratina watched her and scoffed at the woman's inability to see the truth.

During these visits, I would sit on the far side of the room and watch on with wonder and marvel at my grandmother's acting abilities. It was always very entertaining.

Chapter 4

DR. RUEBEN'S TRANSLUCENT skin and elongated frame gave him a sickly appearance. He looked as if he needed a doctor himself. I would have been afraid to see him naked. His penis was probably the size of his baby finger.

"You're looking a bit better today, Miss Jones," he said with a strange accent that I hadn't noticed before.

I scrutinized his etched-out face while he scribbled some notes. Ratina would not have approved of his penmanship.

"How's the head today?"

I felt the bandages. "It's still hurting."

"That's to be expected."

"What do you mean by that?" I asked suspiciously.

"I mean with your head trauma."

I gave him a strange look.

He looked at his watch. "Well, there are a number of things that I would like to try with you. There is no exact science, really, to what we do. We rely heavily on trial and error."

If he was trying to ease my mind, he was doing a poor job.

"Are you willing to work with me on this?"

"I guess," I replied without fully understanding what I was getting myself into.

"I want to see you tomorrow morning at ten. How does that sound to you?"

"What for?"

"For a little chat."

"Isn't that what we're doing now?"

"I want to get into much more detail tomorrow."

"I don't have much to talk about."

"Well, why don't we figure all of that out tomorrow. Someone from the floor will wheel you down. Okay, Miss Jones, I'll see you then."

The next morning the sickly doctor sat behind his desk while I sat hunched over in a wheelchair disengaged and disinterested.

He asked me many questions, most of which I gave a "yes" or "no" answer to. As I watched him scribble an alarming amount of notes, I wondered about the man whose boyish haircut and crumpled lab coat showed no hints of sophistication. I imagined that he had been born a small child, perhaps the runt of his mother's litter, with a nose always in need of blowing. He probably played doctor with his best friend when he wasn't tending to the animals on the family farm. The animals would have been his first patients.

"Now, Mister Pig, you are being rather aggressive today, biting at my boots. Is there something you would like to discuss?"

"Stop talking to the fucking animals and do what you're supposed to do. Is there something wrong with your head?" the doctor's older brother would tease.

"They have feelings you know," the doctor would insist.

"You're out of your goddamned mind. I'm going to beat the crap out of you if you don't get back to work."

The doctor's father would have been just as aggressive. The brother had to have learned it from somewhere.

The doctor's mother would have been his protector and the only one who understood his delicate personality. But she would have been driven to drink and an early grave by her brutish husband and first son. This would have left the doctor defense-less and not well suited for the world. Hence, the confused man before me.

"So, no more voices for the time being?"

"No," I lied. The voices had a way of coming and going as they pleased.

"So, your mother left you when you were two…" he said as he searched through a file folder on his desk.

I nodded my head and looked down. I had no idea what rehashing all that nonsense would do.

"And you were left in the care of your grandmother?"

"What does it matter?" I placed my hands on the locked wheels of my chair. If I'd had enough strength, I would have wheeled myself right out of there.

"It's just to have all the important facts straight. Every detail is important, Miss Jones. I just want to understand your family situation…"

As I listened to the doctor's long-winded explanation, my thoughts went back to Sunday school.

Chapter 5

"STOP MOVING. I said stop!"

I was trying to escape as Ratina forced a scratchy taffeta dress over my head. I was five.

"Stop now! If you can't hear…" She groped for the belt that was never far out of reach.

I gave in.

She knew I didn't want to go to church, but she always insisted and sent me there even when she didn't go herself.

"Come now. Stop dragging your feet like that. You're going to be late for your lesson." Sunday school was usually held after the service, but on special occasions it was held before.

"Be good now," Ratina ordered as she left me at the door of the church. Other children were already lined up waiting obediently for the Sunday school teacher.

When Miss Pierce, a stout woman in her late fifties, finally arrived, she was out of breath.

"Sorry to keep you waiting, children." She pulled the door to the church open. "Come in everyone. Come in now. Let's get started. We have a lot to learn today."

I stood still and watched as everyone filed into the church. When Miss Pierce noticed, she gave me a stern look.

"That goes for you too, Miss Philomena," she snapped.

I looked down at the ground and glanced away quickly as if I was going to make a run for it.

"Don't get any ideas there, Miss Priss. Just get yourself in there."

"But, I'm not well," I said as I tugged at my uncomfortable dress.

"I'm not well—who?" she demanded angrily.

"I'm not well, Miss Pierce."

She folded her arms in front of her.

"Well I don't care how you feel, Missy. You march yourself right in there with the others so we can start the lesson."

I didn't move.

"I said get in there!"

I shook my head.

She grabbed my ear and pulled me inside.

"Ouch!" I cried.

The other children, who had all stopped to watch, now scurried to the front of the church.

She pulled me all the way to the first pews and shoved me down into a seat.

"You see what happens to those who don't hear, children?" Miss Pierce asked as she took her place in front of the altar.

"Yes, Miss Pierce, they feel," all the other children recited.

"Yes, very good. That's right. If you don't hear, you must feel. So now that we're finished with that disturbance, let's begin today's class. Our lesson will be a little shorter today since my brother is the visiting pastor."

"Yes, Miss Pierce," the children replied again in unison.

"Today I want to talk to you about loyalty," she began. "Does anyone know what loyalty is?"

Everyone fell silent. Miss Pierce frowned and shook her head.

"Since no one wants to speak up, I'll tell you. Loyalty is when one person is devoted or faithful to someone else, like we are all devoted and faithful to God. Does everyone understand?"

Everyone but me nodded.

"In the Book of Ruth, Ruth's family had to go to the land of Moab to escape a famine in Israel. But the only ones who survived the journey were Ruth, Naomi, who was Ruth's mother-in-law, and one of Ruth's sisters-in-law. When Naomi decided to return to Israel after the famine, Ruth and her sister-in-law decided to return with her. Naomi, however, urged them to go back home, but Ruth wanted to stay—"

Miss Pierce stopped and glared at me. I was fidgeting.

"Is there something the matter with you, Miss Philomena?"

I looked down at my hands in my lap and said nothing.

"I'll continue then…"

After twenty minutes had lapsed and it appeared that the short lesson was coming to an end, I began to feel anxious.

"So that's today's class," Miss Pierce concluded. You are all free to go and get some air before the service—except Philomena. You will stay here with me."

Everyone jumped up and ran outside.

Miss Pierce followed behind, locked the door, and returned.

"Now why can't you stay still, child?"

I kept my head down and pushed my dress between my legs.

Miss Pierce slid beside me and placed her hand on my thigh. I flinched. The contrast in the size of our legs was extreme. It would have taken five or six of mine to make one of hers.

"Boy, you're jumpy," she said gently, as she reached down and touched my leg.

I turned my head away, shrank back, and squeezed my eyes shut.

"You're not still afraid of me, are you?" Her breathing became heavy as she pried open my legs and inched her fingers toward my crotch.

I covered my eyes when she groped the one part of my body Ratina had told me to never let anyone see.

"Will you be my Ruth, Philomena? Is that it? You want to be my Ruth?" she purred softly.

Tears welled up in my eyes.

A few minutes later, she patted my trembling thighs, bounced up, and acted as if nothing had happened.

"You can go out with the others now." She strolled toward the front door and unlocked it. She would have normally taken out her breast, but I guess she hadn't had time. Its clammy taste was still on my tongue from the week before.

I sat frozen in the pew as my body tried desperately to recover. The impression of her manly hands remained.

"I said you can go now," she repeated. Her harsh tone and manner had returned.

I pulled myself out of my daze and got up slowly. When I got to the door, a large, imposing figure was blocking it.

"It looks like I'm in the way of this little believer," the deep voice boomed down.

I couldn't bear to look the strange man in the face. He looked like a slightly taller version of Miss Pierce.

"Philomena, say hello to my brother, Pastor Pierce," Miss Pierce ordered.

"Hello," I peeped quickly, as I rammed myself between the door and the strange man's leg.

"Who is that little darling?" I heard him ask. "Look how pretty she is."

"Oh, that's my Philomena," Miss Pierce answered nonchalantly.

Out of view of the adults, I spat, disgusted by what had just happened.

That day, like every Sunday, the church service lasted an eternity. The ordeal was made even more unpleasant by the fact that I was forced to stare at a carbon copy of Miss Pierce. I had no idea what he was talking about. All I heard was the happy chirping of birds and the roar of the ocean outside. I kept my arms pressed defensively across my lap the whole time.

I ran home in front of Ratina. In the back room where the cooking was done, I grabbed a rag and rubbed the invisible spots that Miss Pierce had left on my dress and between my legs. I wouldn't dare let Ratina see my shame.

Chapter 6

WHEN I WAS seven, there were two people who were kind to me. One was a teenage boy with one arm who they called Shoppy with the Piece of Arm, or Shoppy for short. Whenever he saw me walking the long trek to or from school, he would pick me up on his bike and carry me in either direction. Ratina had always warned me about taking rides with him. She was afraid we would fall in a ditch and die while he was trying to touch me, but I knew Shoppy was harmless.

At times, I wanted to refuse the rides, but my sore feet always protested and won.

Shoppy would make sure to drop me a little distance from Ratina's house so I wouldn't get in trouble. I was grateful for that.

Each time I rode with Shoppy, he would laugh and tell me about his many girlfriends—how they would spoil him, buy things for him, and "sex him up," as he put it. He always ended his tales with, "What I lack in arm, I make up in charm—Rawhide." That always made me smile. The way he walked like a cowboy was also funny.

One Friday afternoon on the way back home, Shoppy pulled

up behind me with a big grin painted on his face. "Come on up, little one," he said.

I could tell he was excited about something.

"Guess what? I've decided that I'm giving up all my ladies, Philomena."

"Why?" I asked concerned. Shoppy without his many chicks wasn't Shoppy at all.

"I found the one who I'll give up all the rest of them for."

"Are you sure you could do that, Shoppy?" I felt as if we were peers even though he was much older.

"Oh, this girl is worth a million dollars."

"What's her name?"

"Her name is Darlene, and she's the prettiest thing you'd want to see, and that behind of hers is so sweet—too sweet."

"Is she a good person? Does she go to church?" I asked, sounding like Ratina.

"Someone who looks as good as her doesn't have to go to church."

"Are you going to marry her?"

"I already asked."

"What did she say?"

"Well, first she asked me how much money I had and then she said she would have to think about it."

One month later, Shoppy married Darlene. Two months after that, they found Shoppy's body down by the bay. They said he had walked into the ocean wanting it to swallow him alive after he found out that his wife had run off with all his money.

"That Shoppy was a damn fool," Ratina had said. "A damn fool."

I was so devastated by what happened to Shoppy, I couldn't sleep for weeks after. I got through it eventually by singing his favorite country song, "Ring of Fire," whenever I thought of him. Walking like a cowboy with my legs bowed like his was also comforting.

Philomena (Unloved)

The other friend I had was an old woman who had lost her nose because of some disease they said she contracted from kissing a white man. They called her No Nose Lil, but I called her Miss Lil because I didn't want to be rude. Ratina had taught me better than that. Miss Lil was one of Ratina's best customers. It was Ratina who had predicted that she would lose her nose before her sixtieth birthday, and by chance, it actually happened just days before.

Each time Miss Lil came to the house, she would bring a sweet treat. When she gave it to me, she would always pat me on the head as if she knew my deepest worries and wanted to say "Don't worry about anything, child. Everything is going to be all right. You will see that mother of yours someday." I always found her touch very reassuring.

Whenever I saw Miss Lil in the road, she always had a smile for me and would say, "Mind yourself now. Be a good girl." I would always answer, "I will, Miss Lil, I will." I wanted to get close to her and whisper in her ear, tell her about Miss Pierce the Sunday school teacher and what she was doing to me, but I was too afraid someone else would hear. She was the only one I felt would believe me. Ratina, who always spoke highly of Miss Pierce, would have never believed that her church sister would be capable of such things. I kept telling myself that the next time I was alone with Miss Lil, I would tell her, but that time never came. Miss Lil died shortly after Shoppy walked into the sea. They said she had died from leprosy and had never contracted anything from the white man she had once kissed. I found the two deaths so close together very difficult. I cried for a long time afterward. I made sure to go to the outhouse or the bush so that Ratina wouldn't hear me cry.

Chapter 7

I HAD A total of ten electroshock treatments during my stay in the hospital. I didn't notice any harmful side effects at the beginning, but then I started to realize that I couldn't remember what I had for breakfast or if I had breakfast at all. My sexual desire had also dissipated. As the sessions went on, larger chunks of my memory were being erased. I couldn't remember my times tables or how to hold the knitting needles that one of the volunteers had found for me.

"Why don't you try again," the volunteer kept on insisting.

But no matter how hard I tried to purl or stitch, I couldn't. It was as if Ratina had never taught me.

The irony is that I could still remember in detail most of my painful childhood memories. When I asked the doctor about it, his reply was less than satisfactory.

"Side effects are to be expected, but typically they are minor and the benefits far outweigh them," he said. I begged to differ.

On the day of the last treatment, I had to see him in the morning for another one of our chats. It was Friday, and it was raining outside. As I sat there I felt conflicted, irritated by his repetitive questions and calmed by the sight of the rain.

Philomena *(Unloved)*

"Philomena, I asked you a question. Would you prefer if I closed the blinds so that you wouldn't be so distracted?"

"No, please don't close them," I insisted, looking directly at him for the first time.

"Okay, the question."

"What was it?"

"It was about your mother. How do you think not having her in your life affected you?"

"Aren't you supposed to tell me that? And haven't we talked about all of this before?"

"Yes, we've been over this before. I just wanted to hear your thoughts."

"I told you what I thought before."

"Well, please tell me again. I think it's very important. Please, go ahead."

"Well, I think what I said before is that you can't miss what you never had."

"But that's not true. You did have her, and that's not all that you said before. You were far more sentimental earlier."

"I don't remember what I said before. Don't you write these things down?"

He picked up his notepad and flipped the pages backward then forward, slowly at first, then with a bit more urgency. "I can't seem to find that note." He seemed flustered. "But I think I remember you telling me something about the spot on your head."

"I told you that?" I didn't remember, nor did I believe that I would have shared that with him or anyone.

"It was the spot where she kissed you. Do you remember now?"

"Yes."

"So, it sounds to me like not having her impacted you greatly."

How very obvious, I thought. *Couldn't you come up with anything more profound than that?* At times he seemed to have as little insight as a child, even though the degrees on the wall said that he had gone to some fancy universities. *Money not well spent*, I thought.

"Well, what I was really trying to get at was that you saw the pastor as a substitute for your mother."

"No, that would have been my grandmother."

"But she didn't provide you with any of the attention you got from the pastor."

"That wasn't attention. That was sex, plain and simple." If he didn't know the difference between the two things, I really felt sorry for him.

"Yes, yes, of course, but you know what I mean. He took care of you and provided you with things that a mother or father would normally give a child. He made sure you saw a doctor and got medicine when you were sick."

"Yes, but he still wasn't my mother."

"What I'm really trying to say is that, had your mother not abandoned you and left you with your grandmother, you would have never developed the type of relationship that you did with the pastor."

He was right. That was the most sense he had ever made. When he continued with one of his monologues, I watched his narrow face and looked for clues about his life again. In his face, I saw a great deal of pain. I imagined revised scenarios to ones I had envisioned earlier. Maybe his father was very stern, and the doctor hadn't lived up to the old man's expectations. Maybe his mother had strayed and slept with another man. Or maybe it was the father who had strayed. Maybe the doctor had a secret male lover, and it was killing him that they couldn't live out in the open. From the looks of his brownish teeth, I could tell that he drank lots of coffee, had a sweet tooth, and didn't brush properly. His dry lips told me that he didn't drink enough water. The dark patches under his eyes told me that he wasn't getting enough sleep. He probably ate pie or cake with tea right before bed, but his inherited genes kept him slim. The hair growing out of his ears told me that he would soon be an old man. The wrinkles around his eyes told me that he had many regrets—maybe too many to bear at times. Maybe he had dreamed of being some kind of artist—a painter or a writer perhaps—but his parents had convinced him that he had to get a job that could feed a family, buy a house and car, and pay for vacations.

After staring at the doctor for what felt like hours, I came to the same conclusion I had before—that he needed a doctor himself.

When our session was over, the plastic-arms guy came to wheel me back upstairs.

"I'll be back in thirty minutes to take you down for your treatment," he announced when we reached my room.

I didn't bother getting out of the chair; I just sat there twiddling my thumbs and looking out the window at the rain as my mind wavered between the pastor and his promises, the doctor's gay lover, and the orderly's greasy biceps.

The same three people were in the treatment room when I got there. I didn't feel like being lifted, so I climbed onto the examining table myself.

"How are you doing, Philomena?" Dr. Rueben asked, as if we had not just spent more than an hour together a short while ago.

The students were quiet as usual.

"As I told you before, Philomena, today is going to be your last treatment. We think that they have helped a lot."

In what way, exactly? I wanted to ask, but I had no desire to listen to any of his long-winded, uninspired answers.

"We are going to up the dose just a bit, but you shouldn't feel any different."

I had become weary of his claims. The last time he made

such a promise, my heart almost stopped. I was not the only skeptic. I noticed the male student glance at the defibrillator out of the corner of his eye.

"Wait!" I yelled, just as the doctor was about to push the red "treat" button. I caught him by surprise. "Are you sure it's going to be okay?"

"Don't worry, you're in good hands."

I rolled my eyes but nobody noticed.

The button was pressed and my body seized softly at first, then more forcefully. My heart began to race as my body convulsed.

Unable to speak, I gave the doctor a look of panic. He ran to the machine and pressed the blue "abort" button—the same one he had come very close to pushing the last time he had made a false promise.

"It's not stopping," the female student yelled frantically. "It's not stopping."

"Unplug the machine," the male student screamed, adding to the pandemonium.

I shook violently as I watched the doctor bend over and yank the plug from the wall.

"There," he announced.

I shook one last time before falling unconscious.

When I came to, I was back in my room and the doctor was standing over me.

"You gave us a fright there, Philomena." He took my hand in his.

"Me too, Doctor. Me too."

For the next few minutes we stared at each other in silence not knowing what else to do.

Chapter 8

FROM THE FIRST time with the pastor to the second, it was exactly two weeks and four days. I was ten, and the pastor had just moved back from St. Eustatius where he had been filling in for another pastor who had taken a temporary post in England. When the regular pastor at our church got sick and died, Pastor Pierce became the new permanent pastor. He seemed less scary than his sister, who had stopped interfering with me when I was eight. For two years, I was left alone and didn't have to worry about anyone doing anything to me against my wishes. The holiday, however, came to an end one Friday afternoon.

I was sitting and sewing a dress for my straw doll when there was a soft knock at the door. Ratina had gone into town.

"Good afternoon," the male voice whispered. When I opened the door, I saw Miss Pierce's brother, Pastor Pierce, standing slightly hunched over in front of me.

"Is your grandmother in?" he asked, trying to sound official.

"No, sir," I replied, not knowing whether to step forward to block his entrance or step back to let him in.

"Do you mind if I come in? I told your grandmother I would drop by."

I didn't move for a few seconds. Then, with a backward movement of my left foot, I allowed him in. He touched my cheek as he walked by. "You're such a good girl."

I watched him carefully as he took a seat and glanced around at our simple furnishings.

"Can I trouble you for some water?" he asked.

I ran to the back room and poured him water from a jug Ratina kept on the counter.

He smiled at me when I handed him the cup. Then, before I could move away, he brushed his hand across my flat chest. I flinched, then froze. When he lifted up his hand to take a drink, I ran as fast as I could to the room I shared with Ratina.

"You don't have to wait in there. Why don't you keep me company out here," he said, in a tone that wasn't at all like his sister's.

"No, thank you," I said. My arms were now wrapped around me, protecting my tiny breasts or mosquito bites as Ratina called them. My fingers were balled up in fists in preparation to defend myself. I knew I should have run outside, but the bedroom was closer.

"Are you okay in there?" he asked. "What time did your grandmother say she would be back?"

"She didn't say," I answered, hoping that he would become impatient and leave. A few minutes later, the door opened. It was Ratina. I wanted to rush out of the room and into her arms and tell her what the pastor had done and that he was from a family who enjoyed touching little children, but I didn't. I stayed right where I was and didn't say a word.

"Pastor Pierce, welcome. Welcome. I hope you haven't been waiting too long. It's so nice to see you," I heard Ratina say. "I see my granddaughter took care of you."

I listened to see if the pastor would rise from his seat to greet Ratina, but there was no movement.

"Let me go and get some water for myself and then we can talk," Ratina added.

Ratina walked from the front of the house to the back. I prayed that she wouldn't open the door and find me in this state. Luckily, the good host that she was, she returned to the pastor.

"I wanted to talk to you about running some prayer meetings with some of our lost flock. I'm hoping that we can help them find their way back to the church," the pastor began.

Ratina responded enthusiastically. I had never heard her sound so cheerful. I wasn't sure if it was admiration for the pastor or her love of God.

For the next half hour, the two spoke about who the fallen flock were and how best to reach them. All the while, I kept my arms folded over my chest. When I heard the pastor say "well," followed by the scrape of my grandfather's wooden chair, I let out a deep sigh. The ordeal was over. He was leaving.

"Philomena, get out from there now and say good-bye to the pastor," Ratina ordered.

I got up off the floor where I had been waiting, took a breath, and brushed off my dress.

The pastor smiled brightly as I approached. "Such a beautiful granddaughter you have there, Ratina." He stepped toward me, bent down, and kissed me on my head. I wanted to move but I didn't dare. *Blasphemy,* I thought. His lips had landed on the exact same spot where my mother had left her final kiss. I wiped it off, discreetly.

"He means well," Ratina said as the pastor stepped out the door. "He has only the best of intentions." Not wanting to upset her, I kept my mouth shut.

Two weeks later, when I heard some nervous shuffling outside the house, I knew it was him.

"There you are." He smiled.

"My grandmother is not here," I said, hiding behind the door.

"I know. I just passed her on the road. She tells me that you haven't been doing so well with your maths and that you might need some help." Before I could object, he was in the house with the door closed behind him.

"Also, I wanted to talk to you about what happened last time."

I stepped back.

"I just wanted to let you know that there was nothing wrong with what happened. And you shouldn't feel ashamed."

I looked down at my fingers and began to pick at them. I didn't dare look him in the face.

"You see, when two people like each other, they show it by touching one another. It's the best way to express this feeling." He took measured steps toward me. "There's no need to be scared or embarrassed."

"I'm not scared," I said, still looking down.

"Well, you don't need to be. I'm your friend, and you're my friend. We're friends, right?"

I stepped back again.

"I mean, we get along, don't we?"

I allowed my head to nod.

The pastor was now directly in front of me. He placed his large hand on the tiny bone of my shoulder.

I allowed myself to look up at him for the first time. He looked like a bird of prey perched above me getting ready to pounce.

"So, we've established that we're friends. I like you, and you like me, right?"

My empty expression gave away nothing of the torment brewing within me.

He used my inaction as an opportunity to slip his hand down my dress.

I moaned as he groped to find my mosquito bites.

This was the only cue he needed to continue. He undid his belt, tugged my hand, and pulled me into the bedroom.

I dug my feet into the ground but it was useless. He was ten times stronger than me. In no time, he had me on the bed. I closed my eyes while he did as he willed with me. Screaming would have been futile. No one would have heard me since there were no houses for miles. Fighting back would have only provoked him. I had learned that from his sister. When he kissed me again on my sacred spot, something inside was awakened. I wondered if he knew how important it was to me. I believed that he did. Why else would he keep kissing me there?

He pulled his pants back up, kissed my head one last time, and left. There was no blood to wash off the sheet since my hymen had been punctured long before. I lay there dazed and immobile for a short while. Then I got up and opened the window to let out the smell that he had left behind. I also made sure to wipe off the white residue on the sheet with a rag before Ratina returned. Had she asked about the wet spot, I would have told her that I had an accident. I was prepared to suffer her insults, ridicule, and lashes. When the liquid that he had left behind was all gone, I sat in the front room and played with my straw doll. There was no need to reconcile what had just happened. Miss Pierce's interfering had prepared me for it.

"I think you need a new dress," I said as I braided the doll's hair. "You are going to be the prettiest doll on the whole island. Yes you are."

I played with my doll until Ratina returned. We ate dinner and then we slept. My bed was still a bit damp, but Ratina hadn't noticed.

Encounters with Pastor Pierce became a regular occurrence. At some point, I don't remember quite when, perhaps after six or seven months, I found myself growing dependent on them. While Ratina was gone, he was my only company.

When he told me that we belonged together, I believed him. When he cried, "I love you," as he lay on top of me, the words were not impossible for me to understand. I automatically associated it with the feelings that I once had for my mother. He was always kind to me. Never once did he reprimand or speak sternly. His embraces were a welcome change from Ratina's cold distance.

Each night after our visit, I would lie in my bed and replay every moment. I could still feel the indentation of his fingers all along the side of my chest and between my legs. Even though what he did to me was sometimes painful, something inside of me longed for him to do it again and again.

He would come on Saturday mornings when Ratina went to the market and Tuesday afternoons when she led the prayer meetings at the homes of the church's wayward flock. After he helped me with my homework, he took me to the bedroom. When he was done, he spoke to me.

"Do you think you'll pass your exams?" he asked as he lay his head back on my tiny pillow. There was hardly enough room for the two of us in the bed.

"I'm not sure, Pastor Pierce," I said, shielding my nakedness from him.

The pastor looked at me and smiled. "Please call me Paul, or Pauly. That's the name that my mother gave me. I think you will do just fine with your exams. You are a very bright girl." He stroked my face. "I think you're the smartest girl in the parish, and one day you'll be able to go abroad and study. You know, you can do anything you put your beautiful head to."

"Yes, Pastor Pierce."

"Pauly."

"Yes, Pauly."

Chapter 9

"DID THE PASTOR impregnate you, Philomena?" Dr. Rueben asked.

I looked out the window absentmindedly and shook my head.

"Thank goodness for that," he replied.

I said nothing. The doctor's opinion mattered very little to me.

"I think that's enough for today. You must be tired."

I stared at him blankly.

"I should tell you that we've been able to find you a spot in a supervised rooming house. I think it would be the ideal place for you once you're discharged."

I shook my head adamantly.

"What's wrong?"

"No shelters. I don't want to go to a shelter."

"It's not a shelter. It's a house run by people who have some experience dealing with…people…"

"You mean crazy people?"

"No, we don't use that word. I was going to say people who have similar emotional challenges. And you'll have privacy there. I think there are only one or two people to a room, and it's not temporary like a shelter. You can stay there as long as you like."

"I have no money," I said flatly.

"You don't have to worry about that. They'll take care of everything as long as you keep receiving a disability check. They'll take your housing and food expenses out of the check and give you the rest." He got up from behind his desk. "You don't have to worry about that just yet. I'm going to keep you here for a little while still."

As he spoke, I focused my attention on the mist on the window pane. It was my only refuge.

When I woke up the next morning, I noticed a tiny bump on my right arm. At first I didn't think anything of it, but when the bump had doubled in size and was surrounded by a cluster of other bumps by late afternoon, I became frantic. I rang the bell but the nurse took her time coming.

"Can you tell me what this is?" I was freaking out.

"Let's have a look here." She moved closer as she finished the last of her sandwich.

"It wasn't here yesterday!"

"Oh?"

"What is it?"

"It could be some sort of allergic reaction. I'll have to ask the doctor to take a look at it when he comes to do his rounds tomorrow."

"Can't anyone look at it sooner?"

"No, no one is available right now, sorry."

"But it's spreading. Look!"

The nurse examined my arm. "I'm sure it's nothing to worry about," she said as she left.

Philomena (Unloved)

That night, I slept very little. I kept running my hands over my arms and other parts of my body to see if there were any more bumps. They seemed to be multiplying by the second.

The morning nurse almost dropped the breakfast tray when she saw me.

"Oh my. What do we have here? It looks like…. Yeah, I think that's what it is."

I looked down at my arms and legs. The bumps had multiplied even more. So much so that it gave my skin a raw appearance.

"What? What is it?" I asked as I scratched like crazy.

"You shouldn't touch it. Scratching can make it worse."

I didn't stop scratching because I didn't believe that the bumps could get any worse than they were already. "How did this happen?" I said, panicking even more.

"It may be a virus," she said, stepping away from me cautiously.

When the doctor arrived a short while later, he established that it was related to my nerves.

"My nerves? How can my nerves do that?"

His reply was long and convoluted.

"How can I get rid of it?"

"That's a very tricky question."

"You mean you don't know?"

"Well, it's all contingent on the state of your nervous system."

"So there's no lotion or pills you can give me?"

"I wish it were that simple."

He left me in a more confounded state than how he found me.

Chapter 10

I HAD MY first orgasm when I was thirteen. I didn't quite know what was happening to me. The rush of energy that radiated from my pelvic region made me feel as if something inside of me was in the process of exploding and imploding at the same time. I put my hand on the pastor's sweaty chest to stop him for a moment. "Did you feel that?" I asked.

"Feel what? Why did you stop me? I was just about to finish."

"That tingling inside."

"The tingling…oh…you must have come."

"Come?" I asked.

"Yes, like when I finish up." The pastor seemed to enjoy having sex more than talking about it.

"Is it supposed to happen?" I asked naively.

"Yes, of course," the pastor replied.

From that moment onward, I desired to feel that sensation over and over again. When the pastor wasn't available, I tried to seduce boys my own age. When their dicks proved too small, I tried Trevor. Trevor was a year younger than me, but everyone could tell from his height, broad chest, and facial hair that he had already gone through puberty. From his size, I could tell that his wiener would suffice.

"Your beard is coming in nicely," I commented one day after school. I knew that little boys enjoyed flattery as much as little girls.

He touched his chin and gloated.

"Are you going straight home today?" I asked.

He looked puzzled.

I leaned in closer and whispered, "You want to go back in the bushes with me?"

He looked even more baffled.

"What are we going to do in the bushes?" he asked, looking at my breasts.

I could tell he had been propositioned before.

"Just what you think we're going to do," I replied.

We found a spot far from my house so that Ratina wouldn't have another reason to beat the skin off me.

"Take off your pants and let me see if you have enough to please a woman," I ordered the moment we were alone.

He did as I asked and struck a pose with his arms on his waist.

"Very nice, very nice," I replied as I pulled him closer to me.

It didn't take him long to get me to the place I wanted to go. I could tell that he knew what he was doing. His size and technique were more than adequate.

"Meet me here the same time tomorrow," I ordered as I put my school uniform back on.

His smile told me that I could rely on him being there tomorrow or any other day I wanted him.

After only a few weeks of our activities, Trevor arrived at our place in the bushes with a hand full of flowers. I laughed when he handed them to me. They were nothing compared to the ones the pastor had brought for me and given to Ratina.

"I have something to tell you, Philomena." From the stupid look on his face, I knew exactly what it was. I had already heard it from other boys.

"You don't love me, Trevor. You just think you do because I make you feel good," I said, repeating the words I had told the others.

"But I do. I do love you. Look at the flowers."

"I've had nicer," I said, throwing the bouquet to the ground and stepping on it. "Look, I think I'll find someone else to do this for me," I continued.

"No, Philomena. You can't do that. How could you say such a thing? I thought you had feelings for me too."

"Feelings? The only feelings I have for you are the ones right here," I said, touching my crotch.

"Is that all you think about, Philomena? I thought you were better than that."

"Well I'm not, so get lost."

"You really want me to go?"

I turned away from him. There was no need to say anything more.

From that day onward, I made sure to keep clear of Trevor. He did the same. I played around with other boys, but when I got bored, I went back to being with the pastor alone. He was the only one I needed.

Chapter 11

BY THE TIME I was discharged from the hospital, I had been prescribed enough medication to put down a pack of elephants. I didn't want to turn into a zombie so I took the pills only when I felt like it.

The man with the plastic arms wheeled me down to the entrance of the hospital where a cab was waiting. When I stood up, I reached over and did something I had felt like doing from the first time I saw him: I felt his bicep. It was warm and clammy, not at all what I had expected.

"Be well," he said as he waved and pushed the empty wheelchair away. "Don't be a stranger," he added, not realizing how odd his comment sounded.

By the time I waved back, the cab was already halfway down the street. I didn't know if I would see him again, but it didn't really matter.

As the cab drove on, I held my plastic bag close to me. It contained my only worldly possessions: a toothbrush, a few pairs of underwear, one T-shirt, a washrag, a hand towel, and some soap. The oversized pink hooded tracksuit that I wore had been given to me by one of the nurses. My blood-soaked clothes had been thrown out when I arrived at the hospital. The fact that

I would be receiving a disability check that I could use to buy new clothes and whatever else I needed didn't matter much. What I had sufficed.

"I'm sure it's nice to get out," the cab driver said, glancing quickly back at me. He was driving like he knew where he was going.

"Yes, it's nice," I replied, not really knowing how I felt.

My mind was blank as we rode in silence the rest of the way. I attributed the vacant thoughts to my treatment.

When the cab slowed down and pulled over, I yanked the hood of the tracksuit over my head, wanting to hide the bumps that had migrated to my face.

"Here you go. It's that one right there, 274," he announced, pointing to a large old house with a chestnut tree in front of it. A plump white woman dressed in an African outfit stood on the porch.

As I got out of the car, I pulled the hood farther down my head.

The woman from the porch charged toward me as I approached the house.

"You sure you got the right place?" she asked.

"Yes, I think so. The driver said—"

"You moving in today?"

"I guess."

"Where is the rest of your shit, mon?"

The *mon* caught me off guard.

I held up my bag. "Here."

"You lived on the streets?" she asked as she stepped closer for examination.

I pulled on the hood.

"What you hiding under there?"

"Nothing. It's nothing," I said, shielding my face.

"My name is Cindy, by the way. Cindy McMillan." She held her hand out for me to shake. I imagined that Cindy had been fat all her life. She looked like she had been the type of kid who would have begged for a share of someone else's food after she finished her own. Her boobs looked like they were almost as big as her head. Her naked body was probably covered in flaps and folds.

I held on to my sleeve as I shook her hand.

"That's okay; you don't have to worry about those things. I've seen them before. My last boyfriend had them. He was Jamaican. Are you from yawd?"

I shook my head.

"That's right, you don't have the accent," she sang with a big grin.

I felt embarrassed for her.

"Look, don't worry about hiding yourself. I've seen plenty worse, and I have a strong stomach."

I didn't know what to make of her.

"I didn't catch your name. What was it again?"

"Philomena."

"Philawho?" she smirked.

"Philomena."

"Oh, that's different. Is it African?"

"No, I don't think so."

"It sounds African. Look, let's go inside. I'll introduce you to Janice. She's the big boss around here."

"The boss of who?" I asked.

"I was just joking. She's just in charge of running the place. She cooks and tidies up a bit. She's in the office. The house is run by a not-for-profit agency. It has enough room for eight women, but usually there are no more than six of us. Janice works here, but she lives somewhere downtown. We're free to come and go as we please. Janice makes lunch and dinner. Breakfast is usually just muffins, bread, and fruit, but you have to get up early if you want it."

I followed Cindy's large bottom into the house.

There was an overpowering musky smell inside. Drab wallpaper covered the walls, shag carpeting, the floor.

"Do you have animals here?" I asked, with my hand over my nose.

"No, that's just the nasty carpet. I keep telling Janice it should be cleaned, but I guess it's not a priority."

Janice, a manly looking woman, was seated at her desk busying herself with a crossword puzzle. Her neck was broad and looked like a side of beef. A welcome kit that consisted of two towels and a small assortment of travel-sized toiletries sat on a table beside her, along with a few file folders.

"Oh, there you are. They said to expect you around two," Janice said, forcing her mouth into an awkward smile.

I stepped into the office and absentmindedly pulled off my hood.

Janice's smile quickly dissolved.

"Those aren't contagious, are they? They didn't say anything about them," Janice mumbled, trying not to sound insulting.

"Only if you kiss them," I replied dryly.

Janice fumbled through the files on her desk.

"Really, they never mentioned anything about them."

"Don't worry, they're not contagious, Janice. I've been around them and kissed all kinds of them, and I never got one," Cindy interrupted.

"Because if they are, I'm not sure it would be a good idea for her to move in just now."

"They have to do with my nerves," I added. "That's what the doctor said."

"Oh, I see. Just as long as no one can catch them, you're fine."

"Here." She held out the welcome kit.

I made sure to keep a comfortable distance from her as I retrieved it.

Philomena (Unloved)

"Why don't you take Philomena up to her room, Cindy. She's going to be sharing with Susan."

"Oh, lucky her," Cindy replied sarcastically. "Come Phila, let me take you upstairs nah," she added in her best fake accent.

"Okay," I replied, then followed Cindy's large bottom out of the office.

As we walked upstairs, I noticed it wasn't just the carpet that was in need of cleaning; the banister could have used some repairs and the walls a good scrubbing. Ratina would not have approved.

Cindy knocked on the first door on the right. I heard someone speaking from inside the room.

"She likes to talk to herself, that one," Cindy whispered. "Susan, you got company, mon."

"Who the fuck is it? I don't want to see a fucking soul today. And enough with that fucking Jamaican talk. Just because you slept with every Jamaican who ever got off the boat doesn't make you one. Why don't you try talking like a fucking Newfie, Newfie?"

Cindy didn't bat an eye. "Just open up the fucking door and let us in," she demanded. "It's your new roommate, Philomena."

"Philomena—wait! Is that really her name?" The voiced moved closer to the door. "Why didn't you say so before?"

"Open up the fucking door already," Cindy yelled.

The door flew open.

"Do you know that your name means love? Powerful love to be exact. Such a beautiful name. My name is Susan, Susan Pricilla Jane Peters." Susan gave a little curtsy and stuck her hand out toward me.

I didn't budge as I took in all that was Susan Pricilla Jane Peters. She looked like a living, breathing mummy. Her long gray hair had been braided with ribbons, then folded and pinned on top of her head to look like a fruit basket. Her oversized clothes, all the color of mud, were tattered and worn. The deep creases in her face looked as if she survived on a diet of cigarettes and coffee alone.

"Oh, I see. They have you on the hard stuff. It's okay, you don't have to shake my hand. I know what it feels like. What you should do is take a quarter of what they give you. That's what will keep you sane." She touched her chest with both hands. "Your name is so lovely. I wish I had a name like that, but I'm stuck instead with Susan Pricilla Jane. So boring and ugly, don't you think? No poetry or rhyme. I would die to have such a beautiful name. I would literally die."

What an odd bird, I thought.

"Why don't you shut up for minute and let the woman in," Cindy snapped. "Why do you have to be such a motor mouth all the time? I swear you're going to talk yourself to death one day." There was no hint of the fake accent now.

"Sure, come right on in, Philomena dear, and make yourself at home." Susan made a grand rolling gesture with her arms.

The room was surprisingly spacious and strangely girlish because of the light purple walls. There were two single beds placed as far away from each other as possible.

"That's your bed there," Susan said, pointing to bed that was right next to the window.

"This is my side of the room," she added, pointing to her bed, which was covered with a purple blanket. The walls around it were plastered with paper cut-out hearts and a large hand-written sign that read *Manderley*. There were other paper hearts scattered throughout the room.

"You can take some of the hearts on your side down if you like."

I walked to my side of the room and immediately started taking down the hearts and ripping them into small pieces. I could tell that Susan Peters was not pleased.

"What are you doing? I said you can take some down, not destroy them!" She rushed toward me.

Philomena (Unloved)

When I felt her only inches behind me, I turned around and dropped the pieces of paper in front of her.

Susan screamed, "Look what she did. Cindy, make her stop. Make her stop." Susan was now hysterical.

"She doesn't like when people destroy her hearts, Philomena."

"She told me that I could take some down if I liked," I said, defending myself. "You were here when she said it."

"Taking them down and ripping them to smithereens are two different things!" Susan screamed. "Now pick up those fucking pieces and glue them back together, otherwise I'll…"

The loud mouth from behind the door had returned.

"Okay, shh, Susan, no need to take a hairy canary. Calm down. You don't want them sending you back to the hospital, do you?" Cindy covered Susan's mouth.

"But she had no right!" Susan said wiping away tears.

"I know. I know…she was wrong. Can you say you're sorry please, Philomena?"

"But I'm not sorry. I don't like hearts."

"How can anyone not like hearts? What kind of monster are you?" Susan whimpered.

"I don't like them much either," Cindy muttered under her breath.

"What did you say?" Susan asked.

"Oh nothing, never mind. Here, I'll pick them up for you, all right?"

Susan watched as Cindy crouched down awkwardly and gathered the pieces from the floor.

"Here." Cindy handed the pieces to Susan. "Better now?"

Susan gave the reluctant nod of a spoiled child.

"Okay, why don't you two just stay out of each other's way from now on. I think that would be best for everyone," Cindy said before leaving.

I sighed and sat down on my bed.

Susan remained standing. "Sorry for creating such a fuss. I'm usually not that testy about things," she said.

I gave her a cold glare. *All that nonsense for nothing*, I thought.

"I said I was sorry."

"I heard you. My ears work," I shot back.

"I didn't say that they didn't. Well, sorry anyway."

Susan walked to her bed and lay down.

"Once upon a time in a faraway place there lived a beautiful princess…" she began, then paused.

I scratched my head.

"…a beautiful princess who lived in a beautiful palace in a beautiful kingdom."

"What are you talking about?" I asked.

"I'm making up a story."

"Why?" I asked.

"Because I feel like it. It helps me when I'm stressed. The doctor told me that I should find something to do when I start feeling overwhelmed. So I did. I do my stories."

"I don't feel like listening to a story right now."

"I'm not telling it to you. I'm telling it to myself."

"Then why do you have to do it out loud. Can't you just do it in your head?"

"What do you mean in my head?"

"I mean silently so I don't have to listen."

"Stories are meant to be spoken so people can hear them."

"So, what if I don't want to hear it?"

"Then don't listen."

"How can I not listen?"

"Just cover your ears…. In the beautiful kingdom, there were many treasures but the most precious was—"

"Can you just speak softer then?"

"Sure, I'll try," Susan said, and turned her body toward the wall. "…and the most precious was love."

I shook my head as I watched her.

Chapter 12

WHEN I WOKE up the next morning, Susan was not there. She had left a note on the wall next to my bed. It read:

Sorry for the scene yesterday. Breakfast is put away at 11:30 so you should come down by then.

I had no idea what time it was. It felt as if I had been sleeping for days. In the bathroom, I opened the medicine cabinet so that I didn't have to look at my face in the mirror while I washed it. I still hadn't gotten used to the sight of the bumps. It was a good thing they were going away. I felt dirty and wanted to shower, but I didn't feel right about getting naked in the house just yet.

Downstairs, I followed the smell of coffee and found the kitchen. It wasn't far from Janice's office.

"Good morning, sunshine," Susan bellowed out when she saw me. Cindy was seated next to her.

"Finally," Cindy said. "What took you so long, sleepyhead?" She jumped out of her seat. "Look what I made for you." She ushered me over to the stove and took the lid off a small pot. "I used to make it all the time for Trevor Number Two."

I saw a flash of *my* Trevor's naked body in the bushes when she said this.

"He was my boyfriend before last. We're really not supposed to cook here, but we bend the rules sometimes when Janice is not paying attention—which is all the time," Cindy continued.

"What is it?" I asked as I looked down at the white mush.

"Cream of Wheat, mon!" She seemed so proud of herself.

"Sorry, we don't eat that where I come from," I lied.

"Oh, I thought everyone from the islands ate it." Cindy sat back down looking somewhat dejected.

"I told you she wasn't going to like it. It looks like baby Pablum. Who would want to eat that shit?" Susan chimed in.

"But everyone I know from the islands eats it."

"Well not her, obviously." Susan replied.

They both watched me as I selected a muffin from the small breakfast spread on the table.

"And how do you know where she's from anyway, Cindy?" Susan asked. "I'm sure she never told you."

"Well, she looks like she's from the islands. So, I just assumed she was," Cindy replied.

"How does someone look like they are from somewhere?" Susan asked.

"I don't know. It's just the way they carry themselves and how they dress, I guess," Cindy said, stumbling over her words.

"You mean that she looks like she just got off the boat?" Susan jabbed.

"No, I just meant, she has an accent, so I just assumed…"

"So why didn't you say that in the first place?" Susan insisted.

"Shut up, Susan. No one's talking to you."

"I have ears, you know."

"So, you don't want the porridge then, Philomena? I made it extra sweet. Trevor Number Two used to like it like that."

"I'm okay with what I have here," I said.

Cindy sulked.

"Where are you from anyway, Philomena?" Susan asked.

"A very small place," I said.

Philomena *(Unloved)*

"Which island? St. Lucia, St. Vincent?" Cindy guessed.

I shook my head.

"Grenada?"

"No," I replied as I continued to shake my head. "Smaller."

"I didn't know that there were any islands smaller than those. Which one are you from?"

"Montserrat."

"Montserrat. I never heard of the place," Cindy admitted. "It must be really small."

"It is."

"How small are we talking about?" Susan asked.

"Less than five thousand," I replied.

"Five thousand what? People?"

I nodded.

"That's ten times smaller than the piss ass tiny town I came from," Susan said.

"Where was that again?" Cindy asked.

"Penetang," Susan replied.

"Isn't that where that prison is?"

"That's our main tourist attraction," Susan joked. "Was your island big enough for a prison?"

"Yes, we had one," I said with no interest in continuing the discussion. Both women stared at me suspiciously as I picked at the muffin and got lost in my thoughts.

Chapter 13

AT EXACTLY 10:01 a.m. one Saturday morning when I was eleven, I sprang to my feet, smoothed down my dress, and walked to the door. There was no more need to wait for the knock because I knew he would be there.

"How you doing today, darling?" the pastor asked as he stepped over the threshold. His arms were behind his back. "I have some special sweets for you today."

He handed me a small brown paper bag.

"What do you say?"

"Thanks," I mumbled with my head down.

"Now why are you hiding that pretty little face of yours? You know how much I love it. Let me see." He lifted my chin. "Now there we go. You've gotten more beautiful since the last time I saw you."

I forced a smile. As I got older and more accustomed to him, smiling became easier.

"Okay, well your grandmother is at the prayer meeting at Mrs. Anderson's today, so we have about an hour."

He took me by the hand and led me into my room. "I'll look at your homework after." My body went along willingly. It knew

55

what was expected. My spirit, on the other hand, had remained in the sitting room. I would let myself go in sometimes, but that day I didn't.

From my place at the table, I listened to the scuffling sounds from the room. I heard moans and groans and the squeaking of my bed. A deep growl followed by a tiny whimper told me that it was over.

Usually after he was done, the pastor stayed at the house until Ratina came home. Ratina would usually cook something for him; he would eat and then leave. But things didn't work out quite like that.

Just as the pastor was emerging from the room shirtless, Ratina entered the house. Both were jolted at the sight of the other.

"Pastor Pierce! Is this how you help the child with her maths?" Ratina exclaimed at the top of her lungs.

He quickly fastened up his belt and crossed his arms over his chest.

"Mrs. Jones, I thought you were…"

"Mrs. Anderson wasn't well so we decided to have the meeting here. A number of the members of Ratina's group shoved their heads through the doorway behind her. Each looked on in shock.

Ratina stepped forward and blurted, "What's going on in here, Pastor?"

"Oh, I had just spilled something on my shirt and I took it off so it could dry." His uneasiness was not lost on them.

"Where is my grandchild?" Ratina demanded. She sounded as if she was ready to wage war. My spirit clung to Ratina's side while my body was still in the room, pulling on my panties.

The pastor turned his head toward the bedroom as I stepped out holding my dress in front of me. All the women screamed out in horror. Ratina's voice was the loudest. She grabbed the broom and began beating the pastor. The other women followed suit, grabbing whatever they could get their hands on. They forced him out of the house and into the street. Ratina returned by herself after a short while. The ruckus continued without her.

I was fully dressed by then.

Ratina looked down at me with the saddest expression I had ever seen on her face.

"Did he hurt you?" She began to sob.

I shook my head no.

"Has he done it before?"

I nodded.

"Many times?"

I nodded again. She folded over as if she were in physical pain. I started to cry. I couldn't bear to see her so distraught.

"Why didn't you tell me? Why didn't you say something?"

I looked directly at her. "He told me God said it was all right for him to do it. So, I let him." I hung my head again.

"He said God gave him the right to do that? What an evil, wicked man." She wiped away some tears. "What a wicked man."

Ratina took a few cautious steps toward me and folded her arms around me. It was the first time she had ever done that. "What a wicked man," she repeated once again as she stroked my back. Her calloused hand felt like silk on my skin that day. She held on for a long time, then let go abruptly.

"Let's get you washed up, then I'll take you to see the doctor."

"Why do I have to go see the doctor?"

"Just to see if everything is all right."

I could still hear all the commotion that was going on outside as Ratina took me by the hand and led me to the back of the house.

Chapter 14

MY RELATIONSHIP WITH Susan had been strained from the very beginning. Our temperaments were too different. The fact that she rarely left the room, smoked like a chimney, and babbled nonstop didn't help either. The only saving grace was that I found her stories tolerable at times. When I was in the mood, I could sit for hours and listen as her raspy voice took me deep into her strange imagination.

"Did I ever tell you the one about the guy who fell in love with a flower?" she began one miserable December afternoon. We had both been in bed hiding from the cold.

"Did I tell you that one before?" She coughed and repeated her question even louder this time. She always needed to make sure she had an audience, even if it was just herself. I imagined that she was very much loved and spoiled as a little girl. She was most likely some kind of miracle child—like the child that comes after a mother has had many miscarriages—or a little girl that comes after a string of messy boys.

"I heard you the first time, Susan Peters." I groaned and scratched my uncombed hair under my knitted hat. I always used her last name when she annoyed me.

"Sorry, Phil, but I have a good one for you." She flashed me a smile. She knew I hated that nickname. "Do you want to hear it? Do you want to?"

"No!"

"Come on. What else do you have to do? You're just lying there like a bump on a log."

"Why can't you just be quiet for a minute?"

"Please, Phil, come on, be a sport why don't you?" She swung her feet off the bed and sat up. "Come on. You'll like this one. I promise," she said, getting all worked up.

"If you promise to be quiet the rest of the day, you can go ahead," I replied, even though I knew she would probably have to be dead to be completely quiet.

"I promise. I'll leave you in peace for the rest of the day. So, can I go now?"

I nodded.

"I heard this one from a cousin of mine. The guy was a real whack job. He used to collect all of these…"

"Just tell the story."

"So, one day this guy named Nick saw a flower. It wasn't a particularly beautiful flower, just a regular white daisy with a yellow middle. He took a liking to it right away. Over the next weeks, he started flirting with it to try to get its attention each time he passed by. But the flower just acted all coy and cool like she didn't care. This drove him bonkers and made him fall even more deeply in love. He kept on trying. He serenaded and recited poetry but nothing worked. But then one day, out of the blue, the daisy spoke and told Nick that she loved him too. He was so overjoyed, he went home and celebrated by dancing in his room. The next day as he approached his daisy, he saw a man standing and admiring her. When he walked by, he overheard his daisy telling this man that she loved him too. Nick was furious. That night, he snuck up to where the daisy grew and cut her down with some of her daisy sisters. He took them home and threw them into a pot of boiling water and added some spices

Philomena (Unloved)

and made daisy soup. When he was done, he cursed the daisy for having turned him into a cannibal. The end."

"That's it? That's all?" I was thrown off by the shortness of the story. Normally they went on forever.

"Yes, that's it. Did you like it?" she asked.

"Why are your stories always about love?"

"Why do you always ask me that?"

"Because there are so many other things you could be telling stories about."

"So, I like love stories. Shoot me why don't you."

"And I don't think a man could ever fall in love with a flower."

"Why not? A man can love anything he pleases—a flower, a woman, another man, anything that floats his boat."

"It doesn't make any sense."

"It makes perfect sense."

"No, it doesn't."

"Yes, it does."

"You don't even know what you're talking about."

I was beginning to get agitated.

"You don't know what you're talking about."

"You know what? I don't want to start this with you again. It was so peaceful in here before you decided to tell that stupid story."

"It wasn't a stupid story. Just because you didn't appreciate it doesn't make it stupid."

"Of course it does."

"No, it doesn't."

"You know what, Susan Peters, you're absolutely right. You win, okay? I don't want to stay here and argue with you. I've had enough of it. I'd rather go out into the cold and freeze than stay here." I jumped off my bed and grabbed my jacket.

"You know I love you, Phil," she yelled after me. "Now, how about the one about the troll and the princess? That's a good one. Let me see if I can remember it," she continued as if I were still there.

Chapter 15

FOR A SHORT while after my arrival, Janice was very diligent about making sure I took my medication. That was one thing she put some effort into. But much like the others in the house, I threw most of my pills down the toilet. Cindy sometimes sold hers, while others just gave them away. With their varying degrees of madness, most residents kept to themselves. Because of this seclusion, I didn't meet a few of them until after being in the house a number of weeks. This was the case with Heike who emerged from her hiding spot one day.

"Would you like some bread? I just baked it," she said with an odd accent as she greeted me at the bottom of the stairs.

As I stared at the woman's unattractive face and unusually large breasts, I wondered why I had never seen her before.

"I made a sweet kind and a sour one if you like," she continued.

"Sorry. I'm not hungry." I tried my best not to sound too offensive. There was something in her elongated face that gave away her fragility.

"Come, you must try some. It's very good." She walked into the kitchen with her hands glued to her thighs. "Please come."

Philomena (Unloved)

The aroma was warm and welcoming and reminded me of back home, so I followed.

Trays of bread were scattered throughout the kitchen.

"Wow," I muttered under my breath. "You weren't joking."

"Yah, I like to bake. Which would you like to try?"

I looked around the room and then pointed to one of the loaves that had been placed on the kitchen table.

"Yah, that's a good one. I like that one too." She moved quickly to the cupboard and took out two small plates and placed them on the table.

"We should have some tea. We can't eat without drinking, can we? We should have some tea, yah?" The disappointment in her eyes as she cradled the thermos of hot water was endearing. "Sit, sit. You here, and I will sit over there." She looked at me and pointed at two chairs that were across from one another at the table.

As soon as I sat down, she placed the thermos on the table and flew out of the room.

I didn't know what to make of her sudden departure. When she reappeared, she was wearing a pink dress to match my tracksuit.

"Now we can eat," she said as she began to cut the bread. "You like jam?" She swung around abruptly and went to the fridge. Before the jam jar was fully opened, she swung around once again. "Oh, I forgot the butter." She went right back to the fridge. Her quick movements were making me seasick.

"Why don't you sit," I suggested gently.

"Okay, okay, but I forget one more thing. Peanut butter. I like peanut butter, don't you? Everybody likes peanut butter." She dashed toward the fridge one more time.

I watched as she spread butter on her bread, then spooned on layers of jam on top of it.

"My grandmother, Rilke, taught me how to bake. She said the only way to do things was the proper way."

I was heartened by her mention of her grandmother.

"Eat, eat. You must eat to keep up your strength. That's what she would always tell me. When I wouldn't eat, she would beat me. Yah, she beat me good. But you know what? I didn't mind when she beat me. I much preferred it to the other thing."

I just listened attentively as she spread some peanut butter over her bread. I didn't dare ask any questions.

"When she beat me, she messed up my face and made it too dirty and ugly to be seen. She would hide me from them after a beating. Then after two or three days, after the swelling went down, she presented me to them again. 'Isn't she the most beautiful gem you have ever seen? Don't you just want to kiss her all over?' And that's what they would do. They would kiss me all over and do all kinds of awful things to me as soon as the door to the room was closed. I screamed loud and hard the first time it happened, but then the man just beat me, so I learned to be quiet and not say a thing. I was a good girl, a proper girl, my grandmother said. No one was more proper than me, she said. That's why she took me out of school. I was too proper for the girls there at the Catholic school. Much too proper for them, she would tell me."

The more she spoke, the more sullen she became. Her voice also became softer. By the end of her speech, she was speaking in a low whisper.

What she was telling me was making me uncomfortable. I squirmed about in my seat and tried to finish my bread as quickly as I could so that I could escape. The second I finished the last morsel of bread, I sprang up from my seat.

"Why are you going? You didn't have any tea," she said, increasing the volume and pitch of her voice.

"Don't feel much like tea. Thanks for the bread." I took a few steps toward the door.

I knew that she needed someone to talk to, but I had no desire to listen.

Philomena (Unloved)

"Please, I like you. I think we could be friends. Please stay and have some tea with me."

I took one look at the lost look on her face and returned to my place at the table.

"I can see that you're different from the others. I think we could be great friends. Should I pour the tea now?"

"Sure," I said, regretting ever coming downstairs.

"How would you like your tea?"

"Black is fine," I replied, staring down at the floor.

"My grandmother used to like her tea black too." She sighed as she took two cups from the dish drainer and poured out some tea. "She said that was the proper way to drink it. The only way it should be drunk. She…"

"How long have you been living here?" I interjected, trying to get her off the subject of her grandmother.

She stopped abruptly.

"Why you asking me that? Why do you want to know that?" she asked suspiciously. It was as if the person who had offered the bread and had been so open was no longer there.

"No reason," I said quickly. The hostility was palpable. I had no idea what I had done.

"Who told you to ask me that question? I bet it was Cindy. That one is trouble, I tell you. Pure trouble. All she does is sleep with Black men. I wouldn't trust her with anything. I wouldn't give her any of my bread either. She's too fat. It would just make her fatter."

"She didn't tell me anything. She didn't say anything to me," I said, trying to calm her down.

"Then it must have been that bitch Janice. If it wasn't for her, I would have been able to leave here a long time ago and live on my own. But that bitch convinced my doctor that I wasn't well enough. He was willing to let me go, but she found me sitting on my window sill. I told her I was just getting some air, but she didn't believe me. It wouldn't have mattered anyway if I had jumped. I was on the first floor for crying out loud. I would have just broken my ankle or chipped my nail or something. Nothing like what my grandmother did to herself. There wouldn't have been anywhere near that amount of blood. I had never seen so much blood in all my life. I didn't know we had that much inside us."

I stood up and patted her awkwardly on her shoulder.

Instead of calming her, it ignited her. She jumped up and started to scream hysterically. Then she ran out of the kitchen.

A few moments later, Janice appeared.

"What the hell happened in here?"

"I just put my hand on her shoulder and she…"

"Don't you know, you're not supposed to touch her? Didn't you read the sign on the bulletin board?"

"What sign?" I asked. I wanted to ask what bulletin board, too, but I left that alone.

"The one that says: *For No Reason Whatsoever Should Anyone Ever Touch Heike.*"

"I didn't see the sign, and I didn't even know her name was Heike."

"Well, that's no excuse. One of the others should have warned you. Now she's not going to come out of her room for a long time."

"Sorry. I didn't know."

"Well at least she baked this time," Janice said as she looked around the kitchen. "I love this one," she continued as she pulled a piece of bread away from the loaf that had already been cut and popped it into her mouth. "Yummy."

I flashed Janice a dirty look and then left the kitchen. *How could anyone be so callous and uncaring?* I wondered.

That evening as I sat idly on my bed waiting for nothing in particular, Cindy barged into the room.

"How you doing girl?" Cindy asked, sitting down on Susan's bed. "I haven't seen you the whole day. Where you been?"

Philomena *(Unloved)*

I pointed to my bed.

"You spent the whole day here. Why would you do that? Where's Susan? In the washroom?"

"I found a note that said she went to spend a few days with her family."

"Oh, she hates those people. Why would she go visit them? Probably Janice's idea. That woman doesn't have a damn clue about anything."

I was silent.

"So, you just sat here the whole day while the world happened outside?"

I nodded my head.

"Sounds kind of boring," Cindy said.

"I saw that woman who makes the bread."

"Heike? How come no one told me—that's what I was smelling. Did you have some? Was it good?"

I nodded my head.

"She can sure bake, but she's certifiable, I swear." Cindy laughed.

"She's been through a lot," I offered.

"What did she say? You can't believe a word of it. She makes up stories. She's better than Susan with her stories."

"What do you mean?"

"Well, what did she tell you?"

"She told me all kinds of terrible things that her grandmother did to her."

"Her grandmother? She didn't even know her grandmother. What did she say about her?"

"That she took her out of school and made her work as a prostitute."

"Prostitute! I don't think she's had sex before. You see how homely she looks."

"Why would she make up such awful things?"

"She didn't make it up; she just overheard it. That whole

grandmother thing happened to a woman named Isabel from Colombia. She used to live here a few years back."

"What happened to her?"

"Oh, she met some poor guy and got him to marry her. She was a crafty bugger, that one. I wish I could get one of my squeezes to marry me so I could make some more beautiful brown babies."

Even though Cindy tried to appear nonchalant, I could tell the subject of children was a touchy one for her.

"So, what really happened to Heike then?" I asked.

"Nobody really knows. She has a hard time telling the truth or separating what's real from what's not."

"She's not the only one," I replied, slipping into my thoughts.

"Look, I was going to see a friend of mine up the road. You want to come along with me? Some fresh air might do you good."

"No, it's okay. I think I'll just stay here."

"Suit yourself. The guy always has some real good ganja."

I gave Cindy a stern look. "You smoke that stuff?"

"Of course! Can't live without my spliff," Cindy said in her best fake Jamaican accent.

"Later, seen," she added, strutting out of the room.

"Heathen," I muttered under my breath, sounding more like Ratina than myself.

As I lay in bed with my arms crossed over my chest like a corpse, I was suddenly engulfed with the memory of the pastor's scent. It came from nowhere. I held fast to the memory and was not pleased when it faded. I tried to bring it back, but I couldn't. The irony was that I was once repulsed by that same smell. But the loathing had turned to anticipation, then eventually to delight.

Philomena *(Unloved)*

Now it was just plain nostalgia. At one time, I believed what I felt for him was actually love. The vile things that he did had somehow turned into the most beautiful expressions of love.

Chapter 16

THE DAY AFTER the pastor's secret was discovered, Ratina took me to the doctor. Everything was fine down there, and I wasn't pregnant.

"Praise be to God," Ratina had said when the doctor gave her the news.

She then took me to see her old friend, retired Pastor Brown. As I sat opposite him in his fancy living room watching him stroke his white beard, I wondered how speaking to one pastor could help me sort through what happened with the other. It was the last place I thought a sane person would bring me.

I could tell from the confused, almost embarrassed look on his face that Pastor Brown had no idea what to say.

"So, child, did the pastor…did the man…?"

I waited patiently as he formulated his words.

"Did he…ah…ah…touch you in any way?"

I thought, *How can he ask me this question when everyone already knows?*

"Did he hurt you, child?" he asked, correcting himself.

I shook my head.

"He didn't hurt you?" He looked even more confused. "You

don't have to worry, he's not here. You're free to speak as openly as you please."

I pursed my lips and kept my mouth shut.

"Sometimes grown people do things that they're not supposed to do. And those people have to be dealt with. They have to be punished. Your grandmother and some of the other parishioners want Pastor Pierce punished. They want him to pay for what he did to you."

"He didn't do anything to me," I murmured under my breath.

"That's not what a lot of people think. They want me to go to the police…"

"The police?" I panicked. "Why do you have to go to the police?"

"Because what he did to you was wrong."

"He said it wasn't wrong. He said that God would understand. That he had his blessing."

"Whose blessing?"

"God's."

"Is that what he told you?"

I nodded.

"What else did he tell you?"

"I don't know." I turned toward the door to see if Ratina had returned. She had wanted to stay, but Pastor Brown insisted that he speak to me alone, without her influence.

"When did it start? Do you remember how old you were?"

"It was a long time ago."

"How long?"

"More than a year."

Pastor Brown was stunned. "What! And we're just finding out about it now? My God, you poor child. So, tell me how it started, what he did, and so on."

I wasn't allowed to leave Pastor Brown's house that day until

I gave him a satisfactory amount of details. Of course, I didn't tell him everything. There were some things I needed to keep to myself.

The next time I saw Pastor Pierce, he was sitting in one of the two cells in the prison in the capital. Ratina had taken me to the market that day, and I snuck off when she stopped to chat with an acquaintance.

"I'm going to go walk by the sea," I told her.

"Don't stay too long," she insisted. She didn't see any harm in the salt water.

"What business do you have here, girl?" a police officer with a lopsided moustache asked. I was grateful that he hadn't recognized me.

"I want to see someone."

"Someone? Who? People just can't walk in here and see whoever they please at any time of the day like that. We have rules and schedules that we have to abide by, you know."

"I just need to see him for little bit."

"Who is it that you want to see?"

As the officer asked this question, the door to the holding cells flung open, and I saw the pastor seated on a wooden bench looking like he'd been waiting for his death sentence to be carried out.

I pointed at him.

"Him. I want to see him."

"Oh, that man. What is he to you?"

I hesitated. "My father," I lied.

"How could he be your father?"

"He is my father. I belong to his church," I said without faltering.

The officer gave me a suspicious look. "Wait now, aren't you the girl who—?"

I ran off before he could finish.

Philomena *(Unloved)*

When I re-joined Ratina in the market, she was still in the midst of conversation. She never learned of my visit to the jail.

Chapter 17

WHILE CINDY HAD the attic to herself, Amanda and Paula, two women from the West Coast, occupied the other two rooms on the second floor. Amanda was the more interesting of the pair. She had this habit of eating cigarette ashes. I would watch as she put them on her tongue, closed her eyes, and acted like she was eating the most delicious thing in the world. Since she didn't smoke, she had an arrangement with Susan, the house chimney. Each night after the dinner dishes were done, she would come up to our room and discretely pick up one of the two silver pails that Susan used to flick her ashes in. Most times she didn't even say anything—just took the ashes and left.

"As long as she brings my bucket back, I don't give a fuck what she does with those damn ashes," Susan would say.

The agreement benefited Susan as well, since she never had to empty or clean her ashtrays. Amanda usually returned them looking as if they had been cleaned and polished.

"I hope you don't lick them to make them like that," Susan would tease.

The two women forged a friendship based on this partnership. Sometimes I would go into my room and find Amanda

Philomena *(Unloved)*

sitting on Susan's bed gabbing away with her. The conversations would typically come to an end when I entered, and Amanda would leave shortly after that. She never made an effort to speak to me, nor I to her. I guess, had I been a smoker, things would have been different.

Because Susan had "the gift of the gab," as she called it, she would always wait for exactly five minutes after Amanda's departure, then turn to me and say, "You know what she just told me?" Then she would divulge all the intimate details of their conversation—details that I'm sure she had sworn not to tell another living being. Through these snippets of conversation, I was able to piece together Amanda's story, and it wasn't a particularly happy one. None of the stories in the house were. When Susan had enough parts of the story, she spun it into her own tale. She told it to me one hot, sleepless summer's night when there was no relief from the mugginess outside.

"Do you want to hear a story, Phil? This one is not about love, I promise," Susan began.

I had nothing else to do and wanted to get my mind off the unnatural humidity, so I agreed.

"Okay, why not," I said as I mopped my head with my long-sleeve shirt. I never wore short sleeves out of fear that my bumps would flare up again.

"You want to borrow one of my fans?" Susan offered. She got up and pulled out one of three hand-held, battery-operated fans she owned.

"Here you go, sweetie."

I pointed the fan at my chest and reclined. It wasn't very powerful, but it helped.

"Get all comfy now," said Susan. "I'm going to begin."

"Some years ago," Susan started, "in a land not too far away, a baby was born. It was not a happy occasion.

The mother took one look at the child and became sad. During the nine months of her torturous pregnancy, she had hoped and prayed that her child would be born with eyes like hers. 'Please lord, I have suffered enough. Please, let the child's eyes be brown like mine. This is the only way that I will be able to love it. If its eyes are not like mine, I'm afraid of what I may do.' Though she had gotten down on her knees every night for nine months, God ignored her plea. The child was born with blue eyes and fair hair. On seeing this, the mother promised herself that she would never look into the child's ugly eyes.

"From that day forward the young mother kept her promise. She performed her motherly duties—fed, washed, and looked after her daughter—but never once, not even by accident, did she look into her child's eyes. As she grew, the child wondered why her mother always looked away when she spoke to her. The child also wondered why she was the only one in the family with light hair and blue eyes. When the child was seven, she got up enough courage to ask her mother. 'Mother, why don't you ever look at my face? Do you think I am ugly?' The question was unexpected and struck the mother to her core. 'No, my child, you are not ugly. You are a beautiful little girl,' she answered, trying not to cry. 'But why don't you ever look me in the eyes, like you do all of my younger brothers and sisters?'

"The mother was not prepared to answer the question so she ran off into the forest and did not return for forty days and forty nights. While the mother was gone, the little girl went to everyone in the family and asked them the same question she had asked her mother. She began with her father. 'Father, am I ugly?' 'No, my dear, you are not ugly.' 'Then why does my mother not look me in the eyes?' 'She loves you very much, my little one, but your eyes remind her of something very painful.' 'What is it, father?' 'I cannot tell you. This is something your mother will tell you in time. Be patient.' The little girl went to her grandmother and all the other elders in the village and asked them all the same question, and they all gave her the same answer that her father had given her. 'Your mother will tell you in time when she is ready.'

"When the mother returned from the forest, she looked as if she had aged forty years. The little girl took one look at her mother and was frightened. 'Mother, is that you? What has happened to your hair? Why is it gray?' 'I am wiser now, daughter. I visited with the ghosts of the forest, and they instructed me on how to live my life,' said the little girl's mother, looking into her daughter's eyes for the very first time in her life. This surprised the girl more than her mother's gray hair. 'Mother, you are looking at me.' 'Yes, my child. I am no longer afraid.'

'That is good, Mother. I am glad that you are no longer afraid. Can you tell me why you never looked at me before this day and why I am not like the rest of the family?' 'I cannot give you the answers to these questions until you are old enough to understand.' 'When will I will be old enough, Mother?' 'When you are sixteen.'

"So, the girl waited patiently as the years went by. During that time, her mother looked her daughter in the face and told her all the time that she loved her. The little girl felt adored, and even though the family had very little in the way of material things, she felt no one could have had a better childhood.

"The day of the girl's sixteenth birthday was a stormy one. The snow and wind were fighting outside. She had gotten up before anyone else, feeling all the happy excitement of a Christmas morning. When she got downstairs, she heard some rumblings outside and thought nothing of it. Then the noise got closer. It sounded like the voices of several men. 'This one. Let's go in here,' she heard one man say. A thunder of footsteps followed. She stood frozen when the door was flung open.

"A band of strange-looking men with fair hair and blue eyes marched into the house.

"The girl was too frightened to scream. Fear had gripped her tongue. She had never seen such ghosts of men before. They were so pale, they looked like zombies. 'Now, would you look at that,' one man yelled. 'What a beauty. She must have been a gift from someone before us.'

"He grabbed her and forced her down, another climbed on top of her. 'Such beautiful eyes,' murmured the man just before he thrust himself inside of her. 'Such beautiful eyes.' In that moment, the girl, now a young woman, understood why her mother had not looked into her eyes for the first seven years of her life."

And with that, Susan concluded her story.

In my mind, there was no question about it: that was Amanda's story. She had blue eyes and, according to Susan, had lived the first sixteen years of her life on a remote Native reserve. The ashes she ate were most likely one of the many repercussions of her past.

Chapter 18

I HAD ALWAYS detested malls, but like libraries, they became my home away from home and my escape, especially in winter. There, I spoke to no one. I was anonymous and preferred it that way. What I didn't enjoy was watching people eating junk and spending money they didn't have. The kids throwing temper tantrums for candy and toys were the worst. I would have gotten licks had I behaved like that as a child. The only ones I didn't really mind were the old European men. They yacked the day away, spending and eating nothing. The mall was their refuge, their community center and town square all rolled into one. On the most beautiful summer day, you could still find them there.

I would walk around, buy myself a small coffee, and sit for hours. My favorite place was the bench next to a health food store, where there wasn't much traffic. I would sit there and sip my coffee without being bothered. I made sure not to sit in the same spot for too long. I didn't want anyone watching me. I hated it when people watched me. Some people stared at me as if they knew everything that there was to know about me, like how I was born and raised and that I didn't have a mother. Others looked at me as if I were a diseased animal that they would like to take out to the parking lot and shoot. There was one woman who followed me sometimes after I left the mall. I have no idea why she would want to follow someone like me, but when I saw her behind me, I would turn around and go in another direction.

There were all kinds in the mall. The ones who I gave more than a fleeting glance to were the young girls with their little boyfriends acting all grown up, holding hands and kissing. I got to know all the little couples by heart. Their relationships, however, never lasted more than a few weeks. After that, I would see them with a different little boy but up to the same thing. It was all very amusing.

Janice asked me once if I was interested in getting a job at the mall, stacking shelves. That's what Paula and Amanda did two days a week. I refused because the job didn't pay. Instead, the store got paid. That was a form of slavery I didn't want to participate in. When I tried telling Paula that she was being exploited, her reply was, "It's better than hooking on the street." I had to agree. She and Amanda never spoke about that part of their past, but everyone knew that they had both been prostitutes back on the West Coast. I had a feeling that they still dabbled in their old profession now and then. They were always out later than the rest of us who usually came in like children as soon as the streetlights went on. Even though I could be more anonymous at night, I didn't like being out. For that reason, I never stuck around the mall past sunset.

Chapter 19

STELLA, A LITTLE wisp of a woman, came to live in the house shortly after me, but unlike me, she arrived loaded down with four large suitcases. Her droopy face was a real contrast to her expressive eyes. They were so alive that they looked as if they didn't belong.

Susan and I watched from our bedroom window as Cindy greeted her.

"What the fuck do you have in all those suitcases?" Cindy asked, in lieu of a friendly hello.

"Jeez, did you lose your manners in your morning dump there, Cindy," Susan yelled down.

"Mind your own fucking business, Susan Peters," Cindy yelled back, mimicking me.

Stella stood there stunned, not knowing what to say.

"What's all this shit?" Cindy repeated.

"These here are all my essential items," Stella said, sounding more self-assured than what she looked.

"What type of items?"

"Just let her be, Cindy. She has the right to bring as much luggage as she wants. Who died and made you king?" Susan added.

"Where is this stuff all going to go? We only have so much room up there." Cindy had been told that Stella was going to be her roommate in the attic.

"Oh, I'm sure we'll be able to work something out," Stella said as she looked directly at me and nodded.

It seemed as if she recognized something in me, the same way the strangers at the mall did when they glared at me. I wanted to yell *What the fuck are you looking at?* as I did sometimes at the mall, but instead I left the berating to Cindy.

"If it don't fit up there, you're going to have to dump some of that shit in the basement," Cindy continued.

"No worries," Stella replied. "No worries whatsoever. I'll do whatever you like."

It seemed as if she was accustomed to dealing with difficult personalities.

Cindy grabbed two of Stella's suitcases and ordered her to follow. "You better hope it all fits."

"I'm sure it will," Stella said as she struggled to maneuver her bags into the house and up the stairs. Janice was nowhere to be found.

When they got to the top floor, Cindy realized her scolding had been for naught. There was plenty of room. What was troubling her most likely was the thought of sharing her space.

Once Stella had settled in to Cindy's satisfaction, she fell in line with all the other roommates and kept very much to herself.

After a few months of being there, Stella and I had our first and only conversation. It was Wednesday, spaghetti night, and we ended up being the last two at the dinner table. She had been eating silently the whole time, but when Cindy left, she put down her fork and turned to me and smiled as if she was happy to finally have me to herself.

"Janice's spaghetti tastes almost the same as my father's. They make it the same way—with carrots and red peppers," she began.

Philomena *(Unloved)*

I fidgeted with my empty glass as I listened.

"I remember he used to overcook the noodles all the time. Just like Janice." She didn't need any encouragement to continue. It was as if she was speaking to herself as much as she was to me. "He used to have this thing he did with the noodles. First, he drained them in a colander and then poured hot water all over them; then he would put the colander into the pot and turn the stove back on. No wonder they would be overcooked. But they never tasted that bad."

I put the last piece of spaghetti in my mouth and started to stand up.

"Philomena?"

"Yes," I said, sitting back down.

"Why does everyone always do that?"

"Do what?"

"Leave the room when I start talking about him. The doctor says I should try talking about him, but every time I say anything, everyone one just leaves."

"I'm not leaving," I said. I was starting to feel sorry for her even though I had no idea what she was talking about.

"My father loved me. He did. He loved me in his own way. Good or bad, it was love."

I said nothing.

"Underneath everything, he was a good man. He tried hard. He worked hard to provide for his family. He gave me everything I ever wanted…but he took, too…yeah, he took stuff too, but I…I was…He took my…He took my…my innocence. He took my sister…yes, he took my life too. But he meant well. Yes, he hurt us. But we hurt him too. We abandoned him. We let him die all alone in the hospital. I should have gone. I should have been there with him. But my therapist told me that it would be better if I left that chapter of my life alone. I saw him, you know, two weeks before he died, and he gave me twenty dollars to put my mouth on his dick. The man was in pain, but all he wanted me to do was suck his cock a little. It was a dying man's wish, so I sucked it a bit to make him happy. I didn't even take his money. I just washed my mouth out at the bathroom sink and left. That was the last time I saw him. I never told my therapist about that. I never told her that I sucked his dick for old times' sake. I never told her, because it didn't matter. I had sucked it hundreds of times before. It was like nothing. Like eating a Popsicle, he told me. That's what he told me when I was six. 'Stella, do you want to taste my Popsicle?' he asked. He told me that he would give me a quarter if I did it and a dollar if I didn't tell anyone. So, I did it. It was the worst tasting Popsicle I ever had, but it belonged to my father, and he would have never done anything to hurt me. I knew that. He was always looking out for me and my sister and my mother. He was a good guy. That's what he told me. He was one of the best, he would always say. The best damn man you would ever find in this whole wide world, and I believed every single word that he said. He was the best man and the only man in the whole wide world to me, and no one and nothing else mattered."

Janice stuck her head into the kitchen.

"Who's supposed to wash the dishes tonight?" she asked, completely oblivious to the soul bearing that was going on. She had, what I called, selective hearing. She never really discussed any of our issues with us. She felt that was what our doctors were for.

"I think it's Cindy's night," I said.

"Do you know where she is?"

I shook my head.

"I guess I have to go find her," Janice said.

When Janice was out of sight, Stella looked at me with an apologetic frown and continued to talk about her father. Although we shared similar experiences, I didn't think of the pastor once when we spoke. I just thought about what a monster her father had been.

Philomena *(Unloved)*

It turned out, most of the clothes in her four suitcases belonged to him. She kept them because she wanted them close and couldn't bear to part with them or her father.

A short while after our chat, Stella moved out of the house and no one saw or heard from her ever again. I have a feeling she might have moved somewhere up north. She mentioned during our conversation wanting to see the northern lights. It was something her father had always wanted to do but had never gotten around to.

Chapter 20

WHEN THE PASTOR first touched me, I had not started my period yet. When it finally arrived, however, no precautions were ever taken. So at fourteen, four years after he first laid hands on me, I became pregnant. By that time, I was convinced that I was in love with him. He already had three daughters, all older than me, so I hoped that I could give him a son.

My pregnancy was not confirmed by a doctor or by Ratina but by my school friend, Betty, a tall toothpick of a girl. She had suspected that I'd been carrying on with the pastor, but she kept quiet about it.

"Your belly is looking kind of roundish," she commented one day as we walked along the gulley on the way back from school.

"What about my belly?" I asked absentmindedly. I had been daydreaming about meeting with the pastor later that evening.

"It's looking kind of round."

"What are you talking about? Everyone has a round belly."

"Not like that," Betty said as she reached down and felt my abdomen. "You see? It's a bit 'hardish' too."

"Leave me alone," I said, pushing her hand away.

"You sure you don't have something growing in there?"

Philomena (Unloved)

"Something like what?"

"Are you dense?"

I took one look at her grimace and knew exactly what she meant. "I'm not pregnant!"

"Are you sure about that?"

I felt my stomach.

"Well, it does feel a bit bigger."

"It looks like you're at least three months gone."

"How you can tell from just looking?"

"I just can. I've seen many a belly in my time."

"You're talking like an old woman."

"I'm surprised your grandmother didn't say anything."

"She's hardly around, and she hasn't taken a good look at me in years."

"Well never mind that, I'm positive you have something inside there. You better watch yourself," she warned me as she ran up the stairs of her lime-green house. "See you tomorrow."

"See you," I said, but my mind was racing. *Could it be true?* I wondered.

I ran the rest of the way home, dropped my books off, and ran back out into the street.

I couldn't contain my happiness as I caught the bus to the capital and squished myself into the back next to a sweaty old man. I held my stomach and listened to the rumble of the road and the chatter of the passengers all the way to town.

When I jumped off the bus near the town circus, I looked up at the clock. It said 3:30. I was early, but I didn't think the pastor would mind.

Since we had been caught and he had spent a day in jail, our meeting spot had changed to a tiny pink bungalow neatly tucked away in a cul-de-sac in the capital.

As I approached the house, my excitement mounted. But then it stopped. It was the pastor; he was coming out of the house, and he wasn't alone. An attractive lady who looked to be about thirty years old walked out behind him. He turned and gave her a good-bye kiss. Neither of them noticed me as I ran quickly to the side of a nearby house. From my hiding spot, I watched as the woman strolled by looking pleased as Punch.

By the time she was out of sight, I had forgotten my joy. I started toward the house in a fit of anger. The pastor was already back inside.

"Who was that?" I asked, stepping into the sitting room.

The pastor said nothing. The room had an unmistakeable musky scent.

"Who was that?" I demanded again.

"I see you left your manners back in St. Anne's. Who do you mean?"

"The woman that just left here."

"I don't know who you're talking about. The sun must be playing tricks on your eyes."

"I saw you kissing her."

"Kissing who? I wasn't doing any such thing."

"I know what I saw."

"Look, why don't you come here and I'll make you feel better." He adjusted his slacks and stretched his arms out.

"No!" I yelled, rushing back out into the street. "To think I was happy to be pregnant with your child."

"A child? What are you talking about?" He made sure to speak in a quiet, controlled tone.

I turned back around and pointed to my belly. "This!"

I didn't see his reaction.

"Come back, please," he muttered under his breath. I knew he didn't want to draw any attention to himself.

I walked faster.

"Please," he pleaded, sounding more desperate than before.

I felt a pang of pity for him so I swung back around. As I did this, a car sped out of nowhere and knocked me off my feet. I landed farther up the road. Blood was pooling between my legs. The pastor ran toward me but then stopped abruptly.

"Oh my God! Get an ambulance here right away!" he called out to no one in particular.

"Don't worry, you're going to be just fine," he said while still keeping a respectable distance.

All I could say as I lay there with my hand on my belly was, "I'm so sorry."

By the time the ambulance arrived, a small crowd had gathered around me, but the pastor was nowhere to be seen. When the ambulance arrived, the sole attendant kneeled down to examine me.

"Who is responsible for this child?" he asked, looking around.

No one claimed me.

"Does anyone know where this child's parents are?"

"The child is from St. Anne's parish," a woman in the crowd offered. "She just has her grandmother."

"The fortune teller?" a man in the crowd asked.

"Well, if someone can get word to her grandmother, I'm going to take the child to the hospital."

The attendant picked me up and tucked me into the back of the ambulance and sped off.

Ratina shook her head and sucked her teeth when she arrived at my bedside a half hour later.

"Pregnant? My granddaughter? I thought she was just putting on weight."

She had wanted to chastise me for my loose ways, but I could see that the sight of my bandages softened her heart.

"Are you all right, child? You look like you seen death himself."

I was mute. I had no words. The whole time I thought of only two things, the pastor and my mother. I wished that they were both there at my side in Ratina's place.

"Philomena, I'm talking to you child. Are you all right?" Ratina said, waving her hands in front of my face.

She moved her face directly in front mine. "What's wrong with you?"

I didn't blink or move.

"I said, what's wrong with you?" Ratina repeated, this time louder than the first.

A nurse ran into the room. "What's all this yelling for?"

"It's my granddaughter."

"What about her?"

"She's not responding to me. She's acting like I'm not even here."

"That's to be expected sometimes. She just went through a traumatic experience."

"She's acting as if she can't see or hear me. Did anything happen to her eyes or her ears?"

"No, they're just fine. She shouldn't have any trouble with them."

"Then why is she acting this way? I've never seen her like this before. She's acting like she's gone crazy or something."

The nurse peeked at me, then touched Ratina's arm and steered her away from the bed.

"This happens sometimes. I've seen it before," the nurse whispered.

"Seen what?" Ratina demanded. "What have you seen?"

"Mothers getting very depressed after they lose a child."

"But she's wasn't a mother. She's just a child herself."

"All the worse."

Philomena *(Unloved)*

"What do you mean, all the worse?"

"I mean it's to be expected. You just have to accept it and hope that she comes out of it soon."

I knew that my grandmother was there and that they were speaking about me, but none of it registered. When Ratina came closer to me and pinched my arm, I felt nothing.

Chapter 21

INITIALLY I DREADED my visits with Dr. Rueben. I detested the idea of sitting in the room with him asking me the same questions over and over again. Having to stare at his pasty face made it worse. Over time, however, things changed. At some point, I don't quite know when, I started to look forward to the appointments, much in the same way I looked forward to seeing the pastor. There was nothing sexual between the doctor and me, but being in his presence became sort of an escape from the monotony that had become my life. With him, I escaped the house, the women and their moods, the mall, and not knowing what to do with myself. The seat in the doctor's office came to be the only place that I could find some semblance of peace from the world, even if I had to share it with the doctor. Outwardly I gave him the impression that I didn't want to be there, but the truth was, there was nowhere else I would have rather been.

Our sessions usually began the moment I set foot in the door. The doctor would start rattling off questions before I had a chance to take my jacket off or sit down.

"What happened when? How did this make you feel?" the doctor would say jumping right in. Like Ratina, he didn't like wasting time on pleasantries.

Philomena (Unloved)

There was always a long pause between the question and the answer. I preferred to take my time and think through my answers rather than just say the first thing that popped into my head, like the doctor encouraged. Speaking openly about my most intimate experiences didn't come easily. I knew that my reluctance had come from Ratina. She always said, "Don't speak your business in the street." But speaking my business was required during my visits with Dr. Rueben. His frustration showed as he bit his nails down to the finger while he waited. Getting answers from me was sometimes as difficult as pulling teeth. It was all part of the routine.

The order and tone of our appointments were so set in stone that when I walked in one afternoon and asked, "How are you doing today, Doctor?" he became so disoriented that I had to ask a second time. "Are you all right today, Doctor?"

"Yes, of course, I'm well. But our concern is not me, it's with you. What about the voices? Have they returned?"

"No."

"That's good; that means that the medication is working. So, let's go back to the pastor, after you lost the child. When he turned his back on you, what did you do?"

"Nothing. What was I supposed to do?" I was disappointed that I wasn't able to steer the conversation toward him and his personal life.

"He abandoned you. How did that make you feel?"

"How was it supposed to make me feel?" A fly on the window had caught my attention.

"Did it make you feel sad or angry or upset?"

I continued to stare at the fly. It was hopping around the window as if it wanted to come in and take part in the conversation.

"Were you still harboring feelings for him? Were you still attached?" the doctor continued.

It was clear to me that despite his many years of study, he still did not have a clear understanding of the human heart.

Had he been dealing with dogs or cats, that question would have been more appropriate. They have small brains, short-term memories, and are loyal to anyone who feeds them. Humans are much more complex. I wanted to ask how well he had done in school and if he had actually studied human behavior, but I decided not to. I didn't want him biting off one of his fingers on my account. Instead, I waited to see if he would start a lecture about what I could have or should have done if I had been a cat.

"Had he treated you nicely?"

"Nobody had," I replied dryly.

"That's just it. Nobody had been good to you, so that was the behavior you expected."

"It's not what I expected, it's just what I got."

He moved forward in his chair. I sensed that he had been inspired by my answer.

"Now that's exactly it, isn't it? You had no expectations."

As I listened to him dissect what I'd just said, I wondered about the kind of life the doctor was currently living. I imagined that it was no less complicated or traumatic than mine.

Chapter 22

RATINA HAD EVERY right to be worried. I was worried myself. I hadn't said a word since the accident. What was there to say? I was pregnant one minute and not pregnant the next. As I lay in bed next to Ratina, feeling more dead than alive, I wondered what happened to my baby. Was he or she in heaven? Was he or she safe and warm? Did those pearly gates exist for babies who were more frog than human? Ratina had told me once that death was just a long uninterrupted sleep.

"Why don't you just take me right now so I can rest my old bones," she would say.

Then she would cross herself and beg forgiveness for having sinned.

Years before, when I had asked her about death, she had given me a different answer.

"What about heaven?" I had asked

"Heaven? Why are you asking me about that now, child?"

"I was just wondering."

"What did Miss Pierce teach you about heaven in Sunday school?"

"I don't remember," I answered. I had purposefully forgotten everything that woman had ever said to me.

"Well, whatever she told you about heaven, it was all nonsense. All it is, is a story to make people feel better about one day escaping poverty. There's no paradise. It's like they say, ashes to ashes, dust to dust. We come from the earth and that is where we go back to when we die."

"We don't come from the earth."

"Where do we come from, child?"

"From our mothers."

"Yes, of course we come from our mothers, but it's God who gives us life though them."

"We don't grow from the ground like trees."

"No, we don't, but we do come from the earth."

"How?" I asked. Ratina was not making any sense.

"How, well…mother and father and…nature and the earth."

I could tell that she was muddled.

"We just come from the earth because God is the creator, and everything he creates comes from the earth and the air. That's it."

"So, when we die and go back to the earth, what happens to us?"

"We get eaten by worms and bugs, and that gives life to grass, and the grass feeds the cattle, and cattle feeds us."

"So, when you die, you're not going to see Da?"

"No, my sweet husband, may he rest in peace, is long gone. I'm sure he was a bellyful for the worms. I'll never see him again. That's why people say their good-byes on their death bed, because there is no more seeing or doing after we're gone."

"But the Bible talks about heaven, doesn't it?"

"The Bible talks about a lot of things. Some believe every single word, but I can't do that. My mother taught me to never take things at face value. She taught me to believe in goodness and fairness but not to believe everything I read. You know that the Bible has been used by a lot of evil people for their own gain."

Philomena *(Unloved)*

At the time, I didn't fully understand what Ratina was saying, but I respected her ability to see beyond what we heard every Sunday in church.

As I lay there still and mute, a strange idea entered my head. Maybe heaven, if there was one, was the only place where love could truly exist. Maybe I would have to wait until I got there before I knew how love felt. Maybe there were people there who gave lessons on the subject. But if Ratina was right, then there was no hope for love. Maybe love was just as mythical as heaven.

Chapter 23

TIME FLUTTERED BY in a blur. As I went about my quiet life, winter passed and gave birth to spring. The wonder of the melting snow and blossoming trees was, however, lost on me. This could have been a function of my medication, boredom, or melancholy—or all three.

When I awoke on the morning of March 20, my initial thought was to go right back to sleep. However, after seeing that Susan had already lit a cigarette, I decided to get up. There was nothing worse than being engulfed by the smell of her Export A's.

"I don't know how you can do that first thing in the morning—before you even brush your teeth. What a filthy habit!" I grumbled. I slipped out of bed, grabbed some clothes, and left the room.

"Yada, yada. You sound like a broken record. Tell me something new, why don't you?"

I rushed past the mirror and stepped into the shower, closing my eyes as I washed off a week's worth of grime. I didn't even bother drying off. It didn't matter if the tracksuit got wet.

Cindy was coming down from her room as I left the

bathroom. Her blonde hair was in cornrows, and she was dressed in her usual black, green, and gold. I didn't feel like speaking to her or anyone else for that matter, so I rushed ahead.

"Happy birthday, Philomena. How are you today, baby?" she sang out in her mock accent behind me.

I looked down at the floor and pretended not to hear. There were a few baby roaches crawling along the baseboard. It looked as if they were speaking to one another. I heard voices in my head. I imagined that it was theirs, but I knew it wasn't. They were mine. They had returned.

Where is it?

Where is what?

That thing?

What fucking thing are you talking about?

You know exactly what I mean. Where is it?

One of Cindy's slippers flew by me, just missing my arm. "I said happy birthday, Philomena. Cha, didn't you hear me?" she repeated louder than before.

I craned my neck around.

"Were you speaking to me?" I said absentmindedly.

"You see anyone else here?" she said, making hand gestures like a market women from back home. "Yes, I was speaking to you. You hard of hearing?" Her hands were on her hips.

"I can hear perfectly well."

"Did you hear me wishing you happy birthday? You know, Janice got a cake for you. She doesn't do that for everyone, you know."

"That's nice," I replied, still only half listening.

"Aren't you happy about that?"

"Sure, sure, why not?"

"Susan still driving you nuts?" She pushed her slipper back onto her foot.

"Yes, she wouldn't be Susan if she wasn't." I opened the door to my room and stepped inside.

"That woman is so fool fool," Cindy added as she waited outside the door.

"You going for a walk?" Cindy asked when I returned with my thick winter jacket and hat.

"Yes, I guess I am."

"You're going to be hot in that coat. It's nice out."

"I'll be fine," I said, escaping quickly down the stairs. I was relieved when she didn't follow.

Outside the air felt stale, almost as oppressive as it was inside. No one else seemed to notice. The happy birds, excited children, and old ladies in gardens all seemed to be enjoying themselves.

By the time I reached the end of the block, I had already forgotten my birthday. The days of the week or times of day held no significance. The same was true for people. I passed them all without noticing. There was an older Black lady who was in the habit of waving at me whenever I passed her house. Most of the time I would just ignore her, but on the odd occasion I waved back. Never more than that, not even a hello. Sometimes, in order not to see her, I would avoid that route altogether.

I was thinking about going to the mall but my feet had other plans. After an hour of plodding along, I found myself in an unfamiliar park. I walked blindly past the playground. The sight of children playing sometimes made me numb.

I spotted a couple of benches just as my feet were about to give out. One was empty. Two teenagers hung around the other. They screamed and scrambled as I approached.

"Oh, my God! What the fuck was that?" I heard one of them say.

I was used to all types of reactions. If I were them, I would have run from me too.

I sat down, pulled my knitted hat down as far as it could go, then closed my eyes and tried to disappear. I was interrupted by an argument in my head.

So, did you find him?

Philomena (Unloved)

What the hell are you talking about?
Did you find him?
Stop asking me that question. Did I find who?
Him, of course. Who else would I be asking about?
All of that just about him?
All of what?
All that godforsaken yelling.
You, my dear, you obviously don't understand.
Of course I do. Everyone knows how important he is.
So, did you find him?
I wasn't looking for him. Where did he go anyway?
I have no idea. If I knew, I wouldn't be asking you.

I shook my head, trying to expel the strangers, but they just kept gabbing. After ten minutes, however, they were gone. In the quiet, I tried as hard as I could to concentrate and fill my thoughts so that they wouldn't return. I tried remembering things I had forgotten after my first treatment. But it was to no avail; only a migraine resulted.

Had it not been for the intrusion of the rain, I would have stayed longer on the bench. The drops were hurting my skin so I dragged myself out of the park.

"Stay off me. Just stay off me," I said. They didn't seem to be bothering anyone else—just me.

I kept my arm up over my head for protection. When I got to the underpass, I stopped and took a breather. I always felt drawn to one particular area under the bridge.

Chapter 24

MY MOTHER ARRIVED unexpectedly early one Saturday morning. Ratina had told her about the pastor, the accident, the baby, and the fact that I hadn't spoken a word since.

"How are you, my darling?" my mother asked as she prepared herself to console me after her long absence.

I gave her an apprehensive look. I understood that it was her, but I couldn't believe it.

She had been gone so long, I didn't recognize her. What made it worse were the tears obstructing my view. I kept wiping them away, but they kept coming. She looked nothing like the woman I had imagined. The ghost-like apparition appeared lost, broken, barely human.

"It's me, sweetie. Don't you know me anymore? It's me, your mother."

Her sudden appearance unsettled me.

"I would have come earlier but I had a situation I had to take care of. You see my man friend, George—Georgie Porgie I called him because he couldn't keep his lips or anything else to himself—was carrying on with some Spanish woman. Well, one night he comes home and tells me that they were going to get married and he was going to move back to Mexico or

Philomena (Unloved)

China or wherever the hell she came from. I told him good for you—good riddance—just come and collect your junk, but the asshole took his sweet time."

"You don't have to be telling the child all that," Ratina said, walking into the room. "She has enough troubles."

I could tell that my mother was not pleased with Ratina's intrusion.

"That's my child there. I can say whatever I want to her."

"Your child?"

"Yes, my child."

"You just remembering that now?"

"What do you mean by that? I been looking after her. Haven't you been getting the money I've been sending?"

"Yes, I've been getting it…. Come, let's go into the other room."

Ratina took my mother by the arm and guided her out.

Their voices remained loud enough for me to hear every word.

"Then what's the problem?" I heard my mother ask.

"The child doesn't need the money that you send. She needs you. Can't you see that? None of this would have happened if you were here looking after her like you were supposed to."

"None of these things should have happened period. I blame you. If you were taking proper care of her and watching out for…"

"Proper care? I've been doing your job all these years. I told you I wasn't able, but you insisted. I'm still not able, but I can't let her run in the street."

"It seems like that's exactly what's she been doing."

"If you don't want me to look after her anymore, all you have to do is take her with you."

I sat up in bed feeling a glimmer of hope when I heard this. The thought of my mother taking me to America excited me.

"I can't do that now."

"Why?"

"I need to get back on my feet."

I lay back down. My hopes were already destroyed.

"On your feet? What have you been doing all these years?"

"Well everything has changed now. Before I got by on both me and George's salaries but now I just have mine, and it's not enough to support me and a child."

"You found enough money to come down here."

"You made it sound like she was going to die. What was I supposed to do? I had to sell a lot of my things so I could buy the ticket. It's expensive, you know. Why do you think you haven't seen me until now?"

"You should have sent for this child a long time ago. If you had, none of this—"

"None of this is my fault. If you want to blame anyone you should blame your fucking self," my mother yelled. "I don't have to put up with this fucking shit."

"Nice language you learned up there in America."

"I didn't learn it up there. I learned it right fucking here."

"Look, I am not going to tolerate you speaking to me like that in my house. Remember, I'm *your* mother."

I was surprised that Ratina didn't come in the room for the belt. She would have never allowed me to speak to her like that.

"You're not my fucking mother!"

"Listen to me. I will not have you using that language in my own house, and let me remind you that your daughter is hearing all of this."

"I don't give a fuck."

"Look, just take your things and get out of here. I don't know why you bothered to come back here in such a state."

"You want me to leave?"

"Yes, please go."

"Okay, I'm fucking going and I'm never coming back, you fucking bitch."

Philomena (Unloved)

I heard some angry rustling sounds followed by some heavy steps, which were then punctuated by the front door slamming over and over again. I thought I also heard some quiet sobbing but I could have been mistaken. I wanted to get out of bed and run after the mother that I hadn't seen in more than ten years, but I couldn't even gather enough strength to call out to her.

I found out a week later that she had stayed with my dead father's family for a few days before catching a flight back to America. There was no return to the house to make amends with Ratina or to check up on me, nor any attempts to try to repair the damage that had been done. It sickened me to think that I had lost her again. Her sudden appearance and abrupt departure worsened my state. For weeks I lay still in bed, finding just enough energy to blink my eyes. Ratina had to feed me and wash me as if I were a baby again. She even had to put a chamber pot under me so that I wouldn't dirty her sheets. Not understanding what was in my head, she would occasionally yell at me and try to force me out of my stupor, but her mean words didn't work.

After some time, however, I was able to find my voice, and I spoke. "Where is my mother?" I asked, even though I knew that she was long gone.

Ratina was pleased to hear me again. Her response was as expected. "Hush now. Don't you ever talk about that woman in this house again," she said. "Enough harm has been done by her."

I agreed and slipped back to into my lethargic silence, vowing never to bring up the subject again.

While the days passed, I festered away in the musty room. The only thoughts I allowed myself were of the pastor. I wondered why he hadn't come to visit and how he felt about our dead child. To preserve my sanity, I refused to contemplate the two things that caused me the most pain: my mother and my baby.

Betty, my school friend who'd first noticed my belly, surprised both me and Ratina when she showed up for a visit one day.

When she stepped into my room and whispered that she had a letter from the pastor, I felt a jolt of life return to my body.

"Shall I read it?" she asked, knowing what the answer would be.

I blinked twice and gave her the signal.

Dearest Philomena,

I am so sorry that I have not been able to see you during your convalescence. I was terribly sick myself, then I had to travel. When I returned from my trip, I asked about you and was told that you were still suffering from the accident, so I wanted to write you with the hopes that my words would help you feel better. If it is any consolation to you, I am also very sorry about the loss that you incurred. You should know that I haven't stopped thinking about you or praying for you since the day of the accident. I do hope that you will be uplifted by my words and find the strength to get out of bed and get better. If you would like to pay me a visit when you get better, I am usually at the house in the capital on Thursday afternoons after three. Under the circumstances I think that it would be best if I didn't show my face at your grandmother's house. In closing, I wish you a safe and speedy recovery.

May God bless you.

I had to use all my force to lift my arm since inactivity had made my muscles weak. Betty understood right away and handed me the letter.

She smiled because she knew that I would soon be better.

It took several days after Betty's visit for me to regain all of my pre-accident strength. On the third day, Ratina watched in awe when I jumped out of bed and began to dress myself.

Philomena (Unloved)

"Wonders never cease. I see you've come back to life."

"Yes, I'm back," I said, unable to hide the excitement in my voice.

"Where are you going?"

"Out."

"Where out?"

"To town."

"Who do you know in town?"

"A friend."

"Which friend is that?" Ratina asked with her arms folded in front of her.

"A school friend."

"Which of your school friends lives in town?"

"They're visiting there."

"Oh, I see." She didn't sound convinced. "Does this friend of yours have anything to do with that baby?"

I adjusted my skirt.

"You can get up and go to town, but you can't go to school?"

"I'll go back next week," I said, brushing past her.

"I see. I don't think you should go."

I was already out the door.

❧

When I arrived at the house at the end of the cul-de-sac, the pastor greeted me with a large bouquet of flowers. When I saw that he had been expecting me, I knew that Betty had relayed my message.

"Are those for me?" I said, trying to smile. It had been so long since I wore anything that resembled a smile.

"Who else would they be for?" He beamed. "You know you're my best girl. I wanted to make up for not being able to come and see you all that time."

He embraced me. It felt like years since he last touched me. "Glad to see that you're feeling better," he said.

"Thanks…. Thanks for the letter," I replied awkwardly.

"Oh, you're very welcome."

After a short exchange of pleasantries, we found ourselves in the bedroom. Things became more relaxed once we were there.

The relationship resumed. I visited the city once a week, usually after school on Thursdays when the pastor was free. Every precaution was taken to ensure that there were no more pregnancies. The pastor saw that this made me sad so he made it a habit of giving me small offerings of clothing, cheap jewellery, and baked goods to help me forget my loss and ease my pain. Unfortunately, the things he gave me did neither.

Chapter 25

A WEEK AFTER my birthday, I woke up with a horrible headache. My temples throbbed at the sound of the pouring rain outside. If I could have turned the volume down, I would have. The thump of my feet hitting the floor only made my head pound even more.

"You sound like Sasquatch." Susan chuckled. Her annoying laugh was the last thing I needed.

As I made my way to the bathroom, I prayed that someone hadn't finished the aspirin, otherwise I would be forced to go and see Janice. I hated dealing with her. She always seemed so uneasy—like her skin didn't fit right, or maybe it was her enormous neck.

There was no aspirin, so I had no choice but to go downstairs. Janice was easy to find and as predictable as the ticking of a clock. She only seemed to leave her office during meal times. Through the slit in the door, I saw that she was deeply entrenched in her morning crossword puzzle.

I knocked.

"Come on in," she said, trying to sound upbeat.

"Morning."

"Yes, Philomena, what can I do for you?" She didn't bother to look up.

"I need something for my head."

"What seems to be the problem?" she asked without a hint of concern and still not looking up.

"My head is killing me." I made sure to emphasize the word *killing*.

"What happened to the bottle of aspirin upstairs in the medicine cabinet?"

"All done," I answered. Why pills of any kind would be left out in the open in a house full of crazies was beyond me.

"Well, that was the last bottle. I'm going to have to buy some more when I go shopping."

"When will that be?" I asked anxiously.

"In a few days, I guess." She looked up at me briefly, then turned her attention back to her puzzle.

"Well. I can't wait that long." I was beginning to feel nauseous.

"There is nothing I can do about that. Why don't you just go walk it off?"

"Walk off a headache?" I knew she would say anything to get rid of me.

"Yeah, some fresh air might do you good," she added.

"It's raining."

"It might be just what you need."

"Well then, can I borrow some money to buy some aspirin if I go out?"

"What happened to your check?" she asked, glancing up again. I could tell she was beginning to lose the little patience she had.

"Gone, long time ago."

"Well, I'm sorry, I can't help you. You know our policy."

"Yeah, whatever," I murmured, and walked out of the office. I felt a spasm in my brain on the way back upstairs. It scared me. The last time I remembered feeling something like that was right after my third treatment. I remember thinking that I was going to die.

"Are you all right there, sweetie?" Paula asked, stepping toward me.

The only time Paula spoke to anyone other than Amanda was when she was drunk or high, but she didn't appear to be either.

"What is it? What's the matter? Are you all right?" she repeated.

"It's my head." I winced. "It feels like it's about to fall off."

"What did Janice say?"

"Nothing helpful."

"Typical. Maybe you should take something for it."

"There is no more aspirin."

"Oh, I have something better." Paula reached into her balloon-pants pocket and pulled out a plastic baggie with several white pills inside. She took out two tablets and offered them to me.

I looked at the pills wondering where she had got them from. She was known to blow her whole check on booze and drugs. She was lucky that the amount for our room and board was taken out each month automatically, otherwise she would have been homeless.

"What is it?"

"Something the doctor gave Amanda. I guarantee they'll make you feel better. They always work for me. I use them all the time when I have a headache."

"Why isn't Amanda taking them?"

"She says they upset her stomach."

"Well I don't need a bellyache on top of my headache."

"Don't worry, you won't get a bellyache. Guaranteed."

"How do you know?"

Christene A. Browne

"I just know."

I wasn't sure if I should take anything from Paula. There was no way of knowing what she was giving me. One good thing, though, was that I hadn't been taking my own medication so there was no danger of mixing the two.

"Don't worry. It's not poison." She gave me a gentle nudge in my side. "I wouldn't do that to you, Phil. So, do you want it or not?"

Desperate for relief, I opened my mouth and she popped the pill in as if she were feeding candy to a child.

"There you go. You'll be right as rain before you know it. I'm going to the corner store for some pop and chips. You want any?"

I shook my head.

"You sure? It'll be my treat."

"No, thank you."

"All right then. Too bad for you. I may never make that offer again."

I didn't answer; I was already in my room.

I had to shift through Susan's junk in the closet to find my jacket and shoes. I would have complained but she wasn't there, probably in the bathroom.

I walked past Janice's office with my head down. The pain in my head was already beginning to subside, and for some reason I felt like running. I opened the door and set off at a slow jog in the rain.

"Where the hell are you going?" a familiar voice barked after me. "I thought your head was hurting?"

I turned around and saw Paula munching on some chips.

"What, you don't know me now? What are you up to? I've never seen you run before."

I didn't have an answer.

"What's wrong now?"

111

In place of Paula's voice, I began to hear another one.
Don't even look at the bitch. She's not worth anything. Just ignore her. Just keep going. Don't say another fucking thing to her. I swear I'll kill you if you say another fucking word.

I lurched forward and continued on my way.

"What the hell!" Paula said. "Is that the way you treat me after I tried to help you out?"

Good girl, that's my girl. You do exactly as I tell you.

"Come on, Philomena, I was just joking around. Let's just go back to the house together. I'll give you some pop and chips. Come on. Okay, whatever. Ignore me if you like. I know who my true friends are."

After two hours of jogging in what felt like circles, I arrived at a place that I knew well. The bridge itself had not changed but the surrounding area had undergone a massive transformation. The abandoned buildings had been demolished, and the roads were badly in need of repair. This made the area look all the more stark and desperate.

The rain had stopped, but it felt as if the temperature had dropped several degrees. I crouched down and sat on the concrete. It was cold, but I didn't care. My headache was gone but my mind was becoming less and less clear. I started to feel a numbness in my lips and tongue, then needle-like pricks on my fingertips and head. It felt like bugs were crawling in the back of my skull and massaging my brain. If I were dying, I thought, I was going to take Paula with me.

Everything moved in slow motion, swirling around me. I began to feel like I was speaking without moving my lips. Words were not words, just indistinguishable sounds. Vowels and consonants fell into a vacuum of space and time. They echoed and moved around at free will. The silence between them was infinite and deadly. It sounded as if nothing existed. My head was playing tricks on me. I was in the process of continually replaying what had just happened. It was like someone was repeatedly pushing a rewind button in my brain. It was an endless loop. Suddenly, I felt like someone had scooped me up and started swinging me around. It started slow, then got progressively faster and more severe.

What did I just say? I don't want to go home. My words came out in a slur and escaped into nothingness.

Yeah, that's the third time you asked me that. Quit it. What's wrong with you?

I felt my lips move but I only heard silence. I wanted to feel normal again, but I couldn't. The voices took over.

Are you okay there?

Stop acting so crazy, why don't you?

Is this where we live?

I thought I was in a bathroom. How did I get there? I was just outside. I had no memory of moving. It was like memory was being erased every few seconds.

Splash some water on your face. It might do you some good.

I pretended to cup some water up into my hands. The sky began to spin again. I didn't know if I needed to vomit or shit or both.

Can you turn off the lights please. There is too much light in here. My voice sounded as if it were coming from somewhere else.

I closed my eyes and tried to shake off whatever was possessing me, believing that rest was the best solution, but nothing changed. Instead of feeling more relaxed, I became more agitated. The bridge twirled around me as I sank farther and farther into my concrete bed. It was swallowing me alive. I feared my skin would fuse with the ground. I was too afraid to move.

You're going crazy!

But I'm already crazy!

I descended into the cold, and the numbness spread through my body.

Are you shivering?

You're not shivering. You're fine.

How do you know? You can't even see me.

I don't need to see. I know.

Please just come and see.

I already turned the lights off for you.

*I know, I won't ask you for another thing…Please come. I think I'm dying…All right, all right already. I don't see why it's so urgent… So…You're not shivering. Don't worry. You're not going to die…You don't even look…*I began to slip deeper into a dream state.

Sorry. Sorry. What are you sorry about?

Those were the last words. I saw a rotund man carrying a tangle of plastic bags. It was Silas Craig. How he kept his round shape living on the street was beyond me. When he realized the pile under the bridge was me, he dropped his bags.

"Oh, my God. Oh my God. Philomena. What… what…?"

Half unconscious, I didn't reply.

He groped about to find a pulse.

"Good, good, good," he muttered and lumbered toward

the road calling for help. Had it not been for the thick layer of clothes, he would have gotten there sooner.

"Help, help! Someone call an ambulance," he yelled as cars sped by him.

An elderly man in a white sedan pulled over on the shoulder and rolled down his window.

"What's the matter?"

"It's Philomena…she's…she's under the bridge. She's not moving." Silas was out of breath.

"Who is what?" The man got out of his car.

"She's under the bridge." Silas pointed toward me.

"What's she doing under there?"

"She's dying!" Silas yelled hysterically. "Come." He tugged on the man's arm.

The man finally understood.

"Dying! Okay, okay…. You go back and stay with her, and I'll go and call an ambulance."

Silas lurched back toward me. The driver went in the opposite direction.

Silas found me exactly as he had left me. He felt my wrist again for reassurance. There was still a faint pulse.

"You hang in there, kiddo, just hang in there. Someone has gone to get you some help."

I was stiff and still.

"I know you don't want to die under this God forsaken bridge, so hang in there, girl, okay. Stay with me."

Had I been able to speak, I would have reminded him of the terrible thing that already happened there years back when we knew each other better.

Philomena (Unloved)

"You can do it, kiddo. I know you have it in you," he continued.

A few seconds transpired before the ambulance arrived. By that time Silas was terrified it was too late.

"What happened to her?" the first paramedic asked as he rushed with his partner toward me.

"I don't know. I just found her there," Silas explained. "But I think she may have been there overnight."

Not even taking the time to take my pulse, the two paramedics wrapped me in a thermal blanket and lifted me onto a gurney.

"It may already be too late," said one paramedic.

"We'll just have to see when we get her inside," the other replied.

"I don't know why they don't just use the shelters. That's what they are there for," the first one added.

Silas was insulted. "Have you ever been in one of those places?"

Neither of the attendants responded.

Silas said a silent prayer and touched the ambulance before it sped away.

"She's barely alive," one paramedic said.

After a quick shot of adrenalin to my chest, I came back.

In the emergency room, my body was lifted like a slab of beef and placed on a dirty gurney in the hallway.

"We found her under a bridge," one paramedic said.

"Don't think she's going to make it," the other echoed. They collected their blanket and left.

By the time the nurse on duty reached me, my eyes were wide open.

"Well look here. They were plum wrong about you. You just might make it after all." She took my pulse.

I saw twenty nurses in the place of one. Their fingers felt like shards of glass stabbing my wrist. I tried to scream but only air escaped from my mouth. No words. I couldn't take the pain so I closed my eyes.

Yes, rest now. Rest.

Flashes of light flooded the hospital room. The curtain had been pulled all the way open.

"Water, water, can I have some water?" I heard myself say out loud in a gravelly whisper.

When there was no response, I growled, "Water, water, water," as if I had been in the desert for days.

An orderly who was mopping the floor in front of my room stopped and stuck his head in the doorway.

"Do you want me to get a nurse?" he asked.

"Water," I repeated.

"I'll go get a nurse for you. Don't worry, someone will be with you right away," he said, grabbing his mop and rushing away.

A few minutes later, a nurse who looked to be almost six feet tall and just as wide stepped in front of me, huffing. Her presence felt like dancing, flickering flames on my face—such heat.

"Yes, yes, what can I do for you?" she asked.

"Water," I repeated. I had never felt so thirsty in all my life.

"Water. Okay, let me just take a look at your chart to make sure that you're allowed to have things by mouth."

Philomena (Unloved)

With a great deal of effort, she walked to the end of the bed, bent down, and flipped through my chart.

"Well, it doesn't say anything in here about that, so I guess you can have some." She took a breath and returned the chart. "I'll be right back."

As I waited for the big nurse to return, I started feeling a strange radiation throughout my body.

By the time the pitcher of water and cup were directly in front of me, I was paralyzed.

Seeing my stiff limbs, the nurse poured some water and brought the cup to my lips to let me drink. When she took the cup away, I had to use all of my force to shake my head.

"No, don't. More, please," I whimpered.

"Okay." She poured more water and brought it to my mouth. I drank like I hadn't drunk in days.

"You're a real thirsty one, aren't you?"

When the cup was empty, I looked at the nursed and blared, "More!"

The nurse complied willingly. I drank until the pitcher was empty.

"Wow, I've never seen anyone do that before. Are you hungry as well?"

I shook my head. I had no need for food.

"Okay. I'll be back to check in on you after I get done with my rounds."

"Can you please stay?" I heard myself ask. I was suddenly afraid of being alone.

"I can't stay right now, but I'll be back in about twenty minutes."

"Please stay. I would like to have someone here when...I..."

"When you what, dear? You're not going anywhere, child. You're stable now."

"No."

"No, what?"

"I'm not stable. I'm not staying," I said. The moment I spoke these words they flew away, as if I hadn't spoken them.

"What do you mean, you're not staying? You're not strong enough to go anywhere, so don't you dare even try."

"I'm not getting up."

"So where are you going then?"

"I'm leaving."

"Leaving where? Oh, I forgot to tell you, someone from that rooming house was here to see you last night. She said that she would come back later today to see how you are doing."

"Who? Which one?"

"Oh, she had a thick neck. She said her name was..."

"Janice?"

"Yes, Janice. That's it."

Janice was the last person I would have suspected.

"So, you promise me that you're not going to get up? You could hurt yourself."

"I'm not getting up."

"Good girl. It looks like you survived the worst of it. You could have frozen to death out there."

"It's not going to be very long."

"What's not going to be long? Look, if you like, I'll go and see two patients, then I'll come right back to you, okay?"

I felt my breathing get heavier and more restricted as I watched her leaving. Lifting my head upward didn't help.

Don't move. Just be still. It's going to be painless. Then you'll be able to rest forever more, a voice advised.

Obeying, I dropped my head back and gave in to what was happening. My breaths became deeper for a moment, then they suddenly disappeared. I closed my eyes and waited to see what would happen. I felt an unfamiliar tingling pulsate throughout my body. At times, it felt like ants were crawling on me; other times it felt like needle pricks. When the feeling reached my head, I began to get overly anxious and started to squirm. Doing my best to restrict my movements, I suddenly felt an eruption in my chest. Just under my heart—maybe it was my heart, I couldn't tell for sure. It jerked me forward, then back again. Then it suddenly stopped and left me still. In the aftermath, as I lay there, I remember the taste of Miss Pierces' breast. I remember the very first time her brother touched me, and how I enjoyed it so much more than I had with Miss Pierce. I remember being pregnant and how happy I felt, and then the accident. I remember Ratina's embrace after the pastor had been found out. It was the only time I had experienced what love felt, smelled, and tasted like. It was a perfect day.

"My name is Philomena Jones and Jesus died for me," I cried out before my torso became completely rigid, then flopped lifelessly.

Right you are.

I was dead.

When the nurse, who had been held up, returned a full hour later, she was shocked to see my limp body.

"Miss Jones, Miss Jones…" she called out frantically as she lifted up my lifeless hand. "She was right, I should have believed her and stayed. She was right. She knew it was coming."

She closed her eyes and mumbled a prayer.

"Lord, please have mercy on this poor woman's soul who died alone. No one deserves to live their final moments like this. Please have mercy on her soul and watch over her."

Tears began to trickle down her face. A few landed on my arm. Their warmth was comforting.

"Sorry. I'm so very sorry," the nurse intoned as she reached out and touched my face.

The next moment, my body was on the ocean, naked and floating freely. I saw an island in the distance. When my body reached the land, I knew I was home. I had arrived.

The next morning, I woke up under the bridge. My body was stiff and cold and very much alive. I got up, rubbed my hands together, and headed home. As I walked, I thought about all the curse words I was going to use on Paula. I should have never taken anything from her. I vowed never to do it again. I had learned my lesson the hard way.

Chapter 26

"I HAVE A surprise for you," the pastor announced the moment he stepped in the door. It was long past four and he was already more than an hour late. The lateness didn't bother me; I was accustomed to that. What upset me was, it was my eighteenth birthday, and I had been looking forward to celebrating it with him. Ratina had not been well, so I forgave her for not remembering.

The pastor's arms were behind his back. He smiled. This disarmed me and made me forget my anger.

"Guess what I have, my birthday girl," he sang.

"Is it flowers?" I asked grinning. I loved when he brought me flowers all wrapped in colorful paper. I always saved the wrappings.

"No, something better."

"Can I see?" I asked moving toward him.

He jogged playfully around the room, prompting me to chase him.

"Come on, Pauly, let me see."

"Catch me first," he teased.

Catching him was easy. The weight he carried around his middle slowed him down.

"What is it?" I grabbed a hold of his arm.

"Okay, okay, let me go for a minute, and I'll show you."

The second I let go of him, he dashed away again.

I refused to chase him.

"This isn't fun anymore, Pauly."

"Okay, you win." He handed me a thick envelope.

My curiosity was piqued.

"Happy birthday, Philomena. Go on and open it."

Inside the envelope, I found an airplane ticket and a large amount of cash.

"What's this?" Tears began to well up in my eyes. "You're not sending me away, are you? I don't want to go anywhere. I want to stay here with you."

"But you've been telling me that you wanted to leave for so long. Remember you said you wanted to go to America to study nursing?"

My desire to go to America had more to do with my mother than nursing, but I had told the pastor otherwise. The realization that I would have to leave him in order to fulfill this aspiration only sunk in with the sight of the ticket.

"But I can do that here. I want to stay here," I replied conflicted, wiping away tears.

"You'll get a better education there, and if you get a job there you can make more money."

"But I don't want to leave…. I don't want to leave you."

"It won't be for good, Philomena, if you don't want. You can go there, do the course, and come back here if you like."

Where I had only looked for reasons to leave, I was now looking for reasons to stay. "But how will I live? This money is not enough. My grandmother can't…"

"You don't have to worry about a thing. I'll take care of everything. I already paid for and registered you in the school."

"But Ratina won't let me go."

Philomena (Unloved)

"She can't stop you. You're eighteen now. You're an adult. You can make your own decisions."

A million thoughts raced through my head as I stood there. "How will I see you? When will we see each other? I'll be so far away."

"You know, I travel quite a bit. I'm sure I'll be able to arrange a visit every now and then."

"Are you sure?"

"Of course I'm sure. I wouldn't just let my girl go away like that."

I examined the ticket.

"That money is for you to buy what you need for the trip, like a suitcase or whatever else."

"Is this the same city where my mother is?" I asked, trying to resolve my conflict.

"I believe so, but whether she is there or not, this will be a great opportunity for you. Something that could change your life," he said, putting his arm around me.

I was both excited and terrified about traveling so far from home, away from the pastor and Ratina, who wasn't well. This worried me. I knew her church sisters would take care of her, but I wanted to do my part. She had not been the warmest to me, but she was still my grandmother, my only family. I was afraid of how she would react so I waited until she was in good spirits before letting her know.

"I have something to tell you," I said as I sat on the bed next to her. Something I had never done before.

"What is it, child? You're not pregnant again?"

"No, I'm not pregnant. I'm…"

"Still carrying on with the pastor. Yes, I know that already. That's common knowledge."

Christene A. Browne

"No, it's not that."

"Then what is it, child?"

"I'm…I'm…"

"Come out with it."

"I'm going away," I finally admitted. My heart was racing a million beats a second.

"Away? What do you mean away?"

"I'm going to America to study to become a nurse."

"You don't have to go anywhere to do that. You can do that right here."

"I know, but it's better there and…"

"Who told you that?"

I said nothing.

"And who's going to pay for this? I guess I don't have to ask."

I remained silent, fearing that the confirmation of her suspicions would make her sicker.

"Yes, you see, I knew it. It's that big-belly man and all of his dirty money. I bet you he looks like a big fat pig with his clothes off. Is that what he looks like? How could you let that man do this to you?"

I didn't reply.

"Answer me, child!" she yelled. Her anger had peaked.

I got up from the bed regretting that I had ever brought the subject up.

"Speak up and stop playing dumb."

"He said it would be better for me," I replied, concealing the part that I had played.

"I'm sure he said that. I'm sure he told you all kinds of things with that big sloppy mouth, calling himself a Christian. What kind of Christian is that?"

"I'm going in two weeks."

"So, I guess you already made up your mind."

"Yes."

"Why so soon? What's the rush?"

125

Philomena *(Unloved)*

"I have to get there for the start of the semester."

"So, you just going to up and fly off just like that—like your mother?"

"I won't be gone long."

"That's exactly what she said. And you see what happened to her. She only came back that one time, and she didn't even have the stomach to stay. I don't know how I could have given birth to such a thing. She couldn't even love her own child."

"She loved me," I said, even though I didn't believe my own words.

"What kind of love is that? And I guess you think that pastor of yours loves you too?"

"He does." I was more convinced of this even when he gave me reasons to doubt it.

"Ha!" Ratina forced herself out of bed, staggered to me at the foot of the bed, and laughed in my face. "Ha!" The smell of camphor oil was overpowering. "That's not love at all. That's what you call perversion. The old man is a big, old, flabby deviant. I don't know how he can stand up in front of his congregation every Sunday morning and preach about being a good Christian when he has no good parts in him. The man is the worst sinner and hypocrite that was ever born. He should die and go to hell. I should have killed him myself."

"That's not a nice thing to say."

"It's not nice, but I mean it. As sure as I was born, I mean it."

"Well, I'm not changing my mind. I'm going."

"Good for you and that bastard!" she yelled, then collapsed to the floor.

I waited to see if she had fallen for dramatic effect. When she was completely still and said nothing more, I panicked.

"Ratina, what's wrong? What's wrong? Are you all right there?" I shook her arm and she looked up at me.

"Oh, it's nothing at all," she replied, as if she hadn't just collapsed. Her eyes were flickering and she was starting to look pale.

"It doesn't look like nothing. I'm going to get the doctor," I said as I helped her back to bed.

"I don't need any doctor. I'll just rest." She grimaced in pain.

"I'm going to get him," I insisted and then left.

By the time I returned with the doctor, almost an hour later, she was fast asleep. I touched her cheek and she opened her eyes.

"Ratina, your granddaughter tells me that you collapsed," the doctor said, standing over my shoulder.

"I'm still alive, aren't I?"

"Yes, I can see that you're alive. But how are you feeling?" He reached down and took her pulse and shook his head.

My worries increased.

"Let me take a listen to your heart." He took his stethoscope out of his black bag. A look of concern came across his face. "Your heart is not sounding so good, Ratina. I'm going to give you some pills now, and when they're done you can get some more at the pharmacy."

He handed the pills to her and took out a pad of paper.

"Please get her some water."

I rushed out as if Ratina's life depended on it. When I returned, panting and out of breath, I was afraid for the first time that Ratina might be dying. I mumbled a prayer to myself as I waited for the doctor to finish his examination.

"Come, come, and bring the water so she can take one of these now." There was no hint of urgency in his voice. "She should have been seen by a doctor a long time ago."

When I handed the water to Ratina, the look on her face told me that she recognized what the doctor knew.

Philomena (Unloved)

After the doctor left, Ratina fell into a deep sleep. I kept a watchful eye on her the whole night.

The next morning she got up and started her daily routine as if everything was normal. It had been weeks since she had been so active. I was encouraged and frightened at the same time.

"Are you sure you should be doing that?" I asked as she swept the floor.

"Why not? If I can do it, why not do it?" She smiled for no particular reason.

This was unlike her. I thought it might be a side effect of the pills.

"I'm going to cook up some beef stew for dinner. Would you like that?" she asked two days later as she lay in bed trying to recover from overexertion. There was no more discussion about my departure. It seemed as if she had accepted the inevitable and was trying to make the best of the situation. I could see her efforts were exhausting her.

"I can cook it if you're not feeling well," I offered.

"No, no, there is nothing wrong with me. As long as I can stand, I can cook," she said, struggling to sit up in bed.

"Are you sure?"

"As sure as shit," she replied with a flash of her old sourness. "Can you bring me my pills?"

When I brought the bottle, she placed a pill on her tongue, swallowed it without water, then announced, "I'm tired. I am going to lie down a bit longer." She needed my help to recline. She stayed in that position for the rest of the day.

The stillness of the next morning was interrupted when she began to stir.

"Philomena, are you there?" she whispered.

"Yes," I said from the other side of the room.

"Can you get me some water?"

When I got back, she had propped herself up on her pillow. She closed her eyes when I brought the mug to her mouth.

"Good," she said. "Good water." She took one more sip, then her head flopped back.

I was scared.

"Ratina, Ratina, are you all right? What's happening?" I yelled frantically.

She said nothing. Her eyes remained closed.

"Ratina, are you okay?" I nudged her shoulder. "Ratina!"

There was no reaction. When I touched her again, her head sprang up and she looked at me with a haunting alertness.

"My name is Philomena Ratina Jones and Jesus died for me," she said with great conviction.

"Yes, I know," I answered, not knowing what else to say.

"My name is Philomena Ratina Jones and Jesus died for me," she repeated louder. She then closed her eyes and her head slumped back one last time.

I waited for her to wake and continue her declaration, but she said nothing more.

By the time I returned with the doctor, her body was already cold. The expression on her face had also changed. The blank, frightened stare had been replaced by a coy grin that made her look strangely alive. It appeared as if she would turn to me at any second and say something cheeky. I didn't know what happened between the time I left and my return. It was inexplicable. As I examined her face, I began to think that perhaps her theory was wrong. Maybe death wasn't the end. Maybe there was something on the other side. Maybe all those who you loved who had passed before you were there. Maybe there was a heaven and pearly gates after all. From the expression on Ratina's face, I assumed that she was happy, possibly happier than I had ever seen her alive. In her death, she was reunited with her husband, brothers, sisters, children, and grandchildren. I imagined they all welcomed her and invited her to a meal of salt fish and Johnny cakes, with specially made coconut ice cream and black cake for dessert. Whatever it was, Ratina appeared to be in that proverbial "better place." I was sad nevertheless. A large part of me wished that Ratina could have known a sliver of the joy that she now seemed to be experiencing. Her life, from what I saw, was one filled with drudgery and misfortune. The only real pleasure I saw her partake in was the enjoyment of her favorite dishes. But most times, it seemed as if she ate without tasting and lived without savoring.

"I will tell Mr. Ward from the funeral home to come by here in the morning," the doctor said before leaving. The idea of having "the dead people man" in my house was unsettling.

I didn't think anything of being left alone with Ratina's body. Dead or alive, she was still my grandmother. She had raised me and done her best. I hadn't gone a day without food or shelter, and she made sure I was always clean and presentable no matter how little we had. She taught me my lessons and manners and all that I needed to survive. Even though my mother had not fulfilled her promise, Ratina never turned her back on me. No matter how harshly she treated me, she was still my blood.

After the sun had gone down, I crawled into Ratina's bed with her for the very first time in my life. It felt strange feeling her body become more rigid and cold throughout the night, but I was determined to stay no matter how frightening it was. I wanted to keep her warm and safe until the morning. Instead of sleeping, I passed the night staring at her and praying for her departed soul.

In the morning, Mr. Ward crept into the house without knocking. When I turned my head, he was standing there holding a basin. I looked up at him with my bloodshot eyes. He was so alarmed, he almost spilled the water.

"What's wrong with you, child? Get up from there right now! Didn't anybody ever tell you, you're not supposed to lie with the dead? You want something bad to happen to you? Get up. Get up!" He placed the basin at the foot of the bed.

I got up and went to my own bed. From there I watched as he undressed Ratina without batting an eye. I had never seen Ratina fully naked before. I tried to shield my eyes, but I couldn't help but look, no matter how shameful. I held my breath when his hand reached the mountain of flesh that was my grandmother's breast. As he washed them in a circular motion, I wondered just how many men outside of her dead husband had touched them. He seemed to pay more attention to them than to her large stomach that jiggled when he passed over it. When he got down to her private regions, I was forced to close my eyes. That was something I didn't want to see. Her legs and feet were left for last. When he was through, he held out the basin toward me.

"Take this outside and throw it out," he ordered. "Then come back and find me some of her good clothes."

I selected an outfit that Ratina had been saving to wear for the queen's next visit. It consisted of a frilly white blouse, a long black skirt, and a mauve hat. I wanted her to look and feel her best.

By the time she was dressed, Mr. Ward's assistant, a scrappy boy, had arrived with the wooden box.

The box was placed on a stand in the sitting room. The neighbors started arriving immediately after. They brought food and offered their condolences. Ratina would have been happy to see all those who had come to pay their respects. Pauly, his family, and my dead father's people were among them.

"Anything you need, just let us know," my aunt said. "And you don't have to worry about any of the funeral costs; we'll take care of it."

On the day of the funeral, I walked with the doctor and Mr. Ward to the cemetery right behind the horse and cart that carried Ratina's body.

It started to rain the moment we arrived at the cemetery. Ratina had always said that when it rained at a funeral it

Philomena *(Unloved)*

meant someone in heaven was crying. I hoped that it wasn't her. When her casket was placed on the ground, I wanted to put my umbrella over her to shield her from the elements, but I refrained. I knew I was already in Mr. Ward's bad book.

The rain stopped and the sun came out halfway through Pastor Brown's blessing. I took this as a good sign. Ratina was going to be okay. My heart sank when they lowered her into the ground. It sank again after the ceremony as I watched Pauly walk away with his wife and daughters. They were the very picture of a happy family, something I had never known.

Chapter 27

ON A SUNNY Monday morning, I woke up and went directly to the window almost like something was drawing me there. When I opened the curtain and looked down, Heike was standing there looking at me as if she had been waiting there for hours. She waved both arms at me, then pointed to the sky. I gave her a puzzled looked. She pointed again and mouthed what looked like "the sun."

I mouthed back "what," not knowing what had lured her out of the sanctuary of her room.

She made an upward motion with her hand, telling me to open the window. "Look how beautiful it is out here!" she said as soon as the window was open. "You should come out."

"I just got out of bed. I need to—" I started.

"Not to worry, I'll wait for you. I have to share this beautiful day with someone," she insisted. "I made your favorite bread. I left it on the table. You should hurry before Janice eats it all."

I nodded and closed the window. I knew Susan would make a stink if I left it open, even though the room could have done with some airing out. I dressed and brushed my teeth quickly. I felt obliged to make amends. I found no signs of Heike's bread on the kitchen table. Janice had most likely devoured it. I grabbed a blueberry muffin and ate that instead.

"What a beautiful day." Heike greeted me enthusiastically in front of the house.

"Do you want to go for a walk?" I asked, thinking that it would do her some good.

"Sure, that's what I was going to ask you. I always see you walking from my room. Should we go then?" Heike said with a hint of desperation in her voice.

I started to lead the way.

"Not that way, this way," she said as she pointed in the opposite direction.

She skipped off and I followed.

"My mother told me that I was born on a bright sunny day such as this," she began.

Her English sounded stiff and formal at times.

"She said she brought me home in a yellow jumper with a matching hat and sweater that my grandmother had knitted. She said it was the best and happiest day of her life. She called me her sunshine. The best and brightest thing in her life. She said that I was always smiling as an infant and when I got older, I was always laughing for no reason. She told me that I would make up these little jokes and tell them to myself and laugh so hard that she would have to come and check up on me to make sure I was okay."

I listened closely as we walked by the corner store in the direction of the mall. A mother pushing a stroller rushed past us. Her young daughter trailed behind her.

"Can we get ice cream now?" the little girl asked.

"We just had breakfast, Carrie. Come on, hurry up, we're going to be late," the mother replied.

"Ice cream should be for any time of day," Heike interrupted.

The mother frowned at her and pulled the child away.

"Parents don't always know best," Heike said as she waited for me to catch up. "I don't remember laughing the way my mother said I did. I remember the complete opposite. I remembered crying at the drop of a hat. I don't even remember smiling much past puberty. I don't think my mother thought much of it until her sister came to visit and told her that maybe there was something wrong with me because I wasn't laughing or smiling anymore. My mother tried to convince her sister that I was okay, but my aunt kept saying, 'It's not normal, it's not normal.' Finally my mother gave in and took me to see a doctor, and the doctor agreed with my aunt, and he put me on this medication. When I asked my mother why I needed to take the medication, all she said was, 'It's not normal, it's not normal.' And then when I asked what's 'not normal,' she said it was me. I wasn't normal anymore. I wasn't laughing or smiling anymore. I wasn't her sunshine anymore.

"I reminded her that I was just growing up. People don't stay the same all the time. Nobody stays the same all the time. It's not normal to stay the same all the time. But she didn't understand. I didn't want to take the medication, but she insisted. When I refused, she forced me. After only a few months of taking the medication, I started feeling real strange. Stranger than I'd ever felt in my life. I didn't want to live. I wanted to die every day. I would wake up in the morning and think about ways to kill myself. I even tried a few times, but my mother got to me. She always kept a close eye on me because she thought I wasn't normal. 'It's not normal,' she said. 'It's not normal for girls to want to die. You're too young to die,' she would tell me.

"When things got too hard for her, she sent me to a hospital. I was in there for a very long time. They kept me sedated a lot. I didn't see the sun for a very long time. Somehow, miraculously, I managed to get myself out of there. They told me later that I was misdiagnosed and stopped giving me all those pills. I started to feel normal again…. Let's go this way," Heike said, pointing toward a road that led to the highway. It wasn't a road that many people walked on.

"Feeling so-called normal only lasted a short while, though. I had no idea why, and I wasn't going to take myself to any doctor to find out. By this time my mother and her sister were both dead. They died of breast cancer within one year of each other. I didn't think that was very normal either…. Let's stop here for a bit." She stopped on the sidewalk just in front of the highway. She didn't look like she was interested in crossing, so I just stood there next to her as the traffic sped by.

"Don't you want to go to the park or somewhere to sit down?" I suggested gently. I didn't want her to feel I was imposing my will.

"No, I want to watch the traffic. It relaxes me," she said, looking more at ease than I had ever seen her.

"You know, dying of breast cancer wasn't normal. Dying right after your sister wasn't normal. None of that was normal. They weren't normal. I think I was the normal one of the bunch, but they insisted I wasn't. All those wasted years in the institution. I never really forgave either of them for putting me in there and then dying like that. That wasn't normal. You know what I mean, Philomena? That's not normal, right? Don't—"

"Philomena, what the hell are you two doing there?" I heard a voice yell behind us.

It was Cindy. The second I turned around, I noticed a bus approaching. Heike had stopped talking mid-sentence. Something about her silence troubled me. By the time I turned back, I caught a flash of her jumping from the sidewalk into the path of the oncoming bus. The screams that I heard from all directions were blood curdling. I wasn't even sure if I had screamed myself. I just felt my chest heaving as I tried to catch my breath. Cindy ran up and grabbed my arm, thinking that

I was going to follow Heike's lead, but I had no intention of doing that.

"Oh my God!" Cindy yelled. "Oh my God. Jesus fucking Christ. Oh my fucking God."

I didn't want to look at what had become of Heike, but I forced myself to. Her body was not too far from where I was standing. She had somehow managed to get herself right under the tire of the bus. Her head had been flattened, and what looked like brain matter was spread all over the road. The rest of her body looked more or less intact. I was surprised by the small amount of blood. The traffic had come to a stop, and people were standing and looking at Heike's corpse as if it were some sort of undiscovered wonder of the world. Cindy kept on holding my arm with one hand and covering her mouth with the other to muffle the continual flow of obscenities.

Sirens were heard immediately, almost as if they had been called in anticipation of the jump. All I could do was stand and watch on in horror. The screams and sirens had faded or stopped. I wasn't sure.

❧

I knew Janice wanted to blame me for Heike's "accident," as she called it. I also wanted to take some form of responsibility, but everyone else knew the truth. Heike would have done what she did with or without me. I had nothing to do with the demons that raged inside of her. Nonetheless, this didn't stop the assault of words that greeted me when I returned to the house.

"What were you thinking, Philomena? You should have told someone where you were going. Why did you just follow her? Why weren't you watching her?" The news had reached the house in advance of us.

"Why weren't *you* watching her?" Cindy yelled, coming to my defense. "Isn't that your fucking job?"

Philomena (Unloved)

"This facility doesn't operate like that. You ladies know that."

"Maybe if you spent more time doing your job and less time playing crossword puzzles, this could have been avoided."

"I hardly think so. If Philomena hadn't—" Janice began.

Part of me agreed with Janice. The guilt I felt was overpowering. There was little I could do to push it aside, no matter how hard I tried.

"You can't blame Phil for this! If you want to blame someone, look in the mirror, bitch. You and that fucking ugly neck of yours," Susan yelled from the top of the stairs.

Amanda and Paula came out and joined in the melee.

"Now wait a second there, Susan. It's not Janice's fault either," Paula interjected.

"Then whose fault is it?" Susan yelled. She was now at the bottom of the stairs with a cigarette in her hand.

"The doctors who let Heike out. She clearly wasn't ready to leave, but they just booted her out anyway," Paula continued.

"They said she was better," Janice said.

"Look how much better she was. She was all better all over the fucking street!" Susan yelled.

"Calm the fuck down, Susan," Cindy ordered, sounding more riled up than everyone else put together.

I wanted to say that maybe the mother and aunt could be blamed for not believing that she was normal and sending her to the hospital in the first place, but I said nothing. I just listened quietly as the women slung insults and accusations back and forth.

Chapter 28

MY FIRST ATTEMPT was when I was eighteen. It was right after Ratina died and just before I left for America.

I was greeted by an oddly cheerful voice a few days after Ratina's funeral. It said, *This is it. This is the day you've been waiting for.*

It was the first time I had heard any sort of voice. I was alone in the house, so I looked out the window to see who was there. There was no one in sight. I looked around some more, then asked, "Excuse me, please, but are you speaking to me?" Ratina had always taught me to be courteous when I spoke to strangers. It could have been her ghost for all I knew, so I didn't want to offend it.

Who the fuck else could I be talking to? Do you see anyone else in this fucking room?

"Where are you?" I asked as I continued looking around the house.

Ratina never used that type of language so I knew it couldn't have been her.

Where the hell do you think I am?

"I don't know. How am I supposed to know? I don't even know who you are."

I came to help you out.

"Help me out with what?"

You know exactly what I'm here for. You asked me to come.

"I asked you to help me do what?"

You know. End it.

"End what? What are you talking about?"

End your life, Philomena. Like you want to—end the long, miserable, sad thing that you call your life.

"But, but—"

But nothing. Let's just get to it.

"What do you mean *get to it*?"

Are you stupid or something? Let's just get on with it. Go and get those pills that Ratina left behind.

"I'm not taking Ratina's pills. I don't know what they'll do to me."

They just might do what you want them to do.

"What do I want them to do?"

Stop with the stupid act.

"I'm not acting."

Then you actually are stupid?

"No, I'm not stupid."

It sure sounds like it.

"Okay, just shut up a second. I'll get them." I rummaged through Ratina's chest of drawers and found the pills. "I got them."

Yeah, I see that. Now take them.

She needs some water, another voice interrupted.

Water is for sissies. She doesn't need water to take them. She can take them just like that.

What if she chokes?

Who cares if she chokes? She wants to die anyway.

"I don't want to die."

Yes, you do, Philomena. You've wanted to die since that first time, maybe even before then.

"I don't want to—"

Just admit the truth, Philomena. You do.

I paused for a second and looked at the bottle in my hand.

So, go ahead then. Do it, Philomena.

Go ahead. It won't hurt. And after you're done, you won't have to think about any of those horrible things again.

I knew the voice was right so I popped the lid off of the bottle and emptied Ratina's pills into my mouth. I had to force them down my throat. When I had swallowed all of them, I got back into my bed.

"Now what?" I asked naively.

Now you just wait.

I closed my eyes and prayed.

"Dear God, please take me from this life and the life from me and please let it be as painless as possible."

I fell asleep while I waited.

The next morning, to my disappointment, I was still very much alive. Ratina's prescription had had zero effect. What I didn't know was that the doctor had given her a placebo. The same drugs that had caused Ratina's death had postponed mine.

Chapter 29

HEIKE'S WAS THE first funeral that I ever attended in America. It wasn't any different from the ones back home. The mood was somber, everyone was dressed in dark colors, and the handkerchiefs and Kleenex were in abundance. The casket this time, however, was closed for obvious reasons.

Guilt ridden, I sat in the back row between Susan and Cindy. I think they purposely sandwiched me like that to protect me from myself and Janice, who had not yet arrived. They had been watching out for her the whole time. This was the first time I had ever seen Susan wearing anything other than her worn-out clothes. She had unearthed a loose-fitting black dress and a pair of black flats. Where she kept them, God only knows. Cindy, the Jamaican princess, had toned down her bright colors considerably for the occasion. She wore a cream-color blouse and black slacks. Her blonde hair was worn straight down without a hat or wrap, which was very unusual for her. Everyone from the rooming house looked their best that day. I wore a black sweater and dressy jeans that I had bought from the secondhand store a few days after Heike's incident. Aside from us, there weren't very many other people. I assumed her family was most likely still back in Denmark or Sweden or wherever she came from.

"Where the hell is Janice?" Susan said. Her eyes had been on the door since we arrived. "She should be here by now. They are about to start. Doesn't that woman have any respect for the dead?"

"She doesn't have any for the living; why would she have any for the dead?" Cindy replied.

"All I know is that she better bring that big neck of hers here before we leave for the cemetery," Susan added.

Just as this was said, Janice walked in with a stocky man who I assumed was the funeral director from the black gloves he wore. Everyone watched them as they walked to the front of the room. Janice was wearing a brown form-fitting dress. This was a big improvement over her regular jeans and sweatshirts. Even though the cut of the dress accentuated her broad neck, this was the first time she appeared even remotely feminine. Susan's and Cindy's lowered jaws showed that they were just as surprised as I was.

"First of all, I want to thank you all for coming out to celebrate the life of this young woman, Heike Sommer, who was taken from us too soon. Janice Goode, a woman who works at the rooming house where Miss Sommer lived, has agreed to take over the program for today. Let's welcome her," the funeral director said.

There was light applause. Neither Cindy nor Susan joined in.

Janice looked out into the small crowd and touched her chest. I'm sure she was feeling a bit overexposed. She cleared her throat and began.

"I was very pleased to be asked by Heike's family to play this role today. Heike was a very special person with many talents," Janice began. Her voice was already breaking. "My first day at the house actually coincided with Heike's first day there. After she settled into her room, she came and asked me if we had any flour. 'Flour?' I said. I found it a very strange request and asked her why she needed flour. 'To make bread of course—what else do you do with flour?' she said. She told me that she had learned to make bread from her grandmother when she was very little, and that's what she did in the house. Hers was the bread that the ladies loved the most. I understood why because I had the pleasure of tasting it, and it was always excellent. On the last day of her life, Heike had actually made some raisin bread—one of my all-time favorites, and it was delicious as usual." Janice began to sob. "Sorry, I'll try to control the tears…. That raisin bread was actually the best she had ever…" Unable to control herself, Janice broke down crying. I was shocked to see her so emotional. I was certain that the rest of the women from the house felt the same way.

"It takes a weirdo to get so worked up about bread. Who does she think she's eulogizing—a baker?" Susan said under her breath. Cindy reached across my chest and nudged her.

"I'm so very sorry for this," said Janice. "I'm wondering if Ana, Heike's mother, could please come up and continue things for me." A tall, slim woman seated in the first row stood up slowly and walked to the podium. Another woman, who bore a striking resemblance to her, followed behind.

I was baffled as I watched them. Heike had lied to me. Her mother and aunt weren't dead.

"My daughter was my sunshine," Heike's mother began.

"She was for all of us our sunshine," the woman beside her added.

"This is my sister, Hanna."

"Yes, she was a very happy child, always smiling and cheery. Always making jokes and laughing at them. That's who she was for the first nine or ten years of her life…"

As I listened to Heike's mother speak, I was able to get a better understanding of who Heike really was and what she had been up against. Heike was not a liar. She was just terribly sick. On that last day, she had spoken some truth. Maybe it was her only truth. Maybe everything else was vague. Maybe, in her mind, her mother and her aunt were dead simply because they had abandoned her right when she needed them most. Reflecting on this helped me displace my own guilt. My invitation had not killed Heike; my lack of attention had not killed her either. She had killed herself, and she would have done it had I been there or not.

At the burial later that afternoon, the cloudless sky provided no consolation to the crowd that gathered. I watched as Heike's mother and aunt clung to each other for support. The weeping willows above them appeared to be hanging their branches in a show of solidarity. I could tell that they were both feeling the weight of Heike's loss, even though only one of them had given birth to her. It was clear that they were very close and loved Heike very much. I wished, at that moment, that I was Heike and that they belonged to me.

There was plenty to eat back at the house. I watched Heike's mother and aunt from a distance the whole afternoon. When they started walking toward me, I froze.

"How do you do?" Heike's mother asked as a hand stretched out to greet me. The two women were so entwined, I wasn't sure who it belonged to.

"Okay, I guess. How are you?" I answered, wanting to flee.

"Coping the best we can, under the circumstances. We heard that you were there when it happened," the aunt replied.

I looked down, unable to look either of them in the eye.

"You poor dear. We also heard that you were liked very much by Heike. You were probably her favorite in the house," Ana said.

This was news to me.

"Yes, Janice said that you had been good for Heike and that you two spoke all the time and she liked to indulge you with her bread," Hanna added.

Susan's story-telling skills must have rubbed off on Janice, I thought.

"I just wanted to tell you that it gives me great comfort to know that Heike had a friend and that you were there in her final hour." Ana untangled herself from her sister and embraced me. Her scent was sweet, almost fruit-like.

"Heike always had nice things to say about both of you," I added. I figured a lie was much better than the truth under the circumstances.

Chapter 30

IN THE WEEKS following Heike's death, I noticed some changes in Janice. She became more attentive. She did fewer crossword puzzles and made more of an effort to eat her meals with us in the kitchen. Also, the door to her office was always left wide open. I assumed her actions were due to guilt.

Her new approach also included the initiation of group activities—something we tried to avoid since the majority of us preferred solitude. The first initiative was a chess tournament. She set up a couple of chess boards in the TV room and made a large sign to remind us. When no one showed up, she was forced to seek us out.

"Come on, guys, it's seven o'clock—time for the tournament," she announced just outside my bedroom door. Susan and I were lounging as usual.

"What the fuck is she doing up here knocking on the doors—is there a fire or something?" Susan sneered. She was in a particularly sour mood.

"She wants us to go downstairs for the tournament."

"What fucking tournament? I don't know how to play tennis, and how the fuck are we going to see to play. It's getting dark out there."

Philomena (Unloved)

"Not tennis, chess."

"Who told her I wanted to play chess?"

"Are you guys coming down? I'm all set up downstairs," Janice said, lingering in the hallway.

"Why don't you go play with your fucking self!" Susan yelled. "And leave us the fuck alone, you witch. Since when did this become fucking kindergarten?"

"I thought it would be something fun to do," Janice said, sounding more sympathetic than usual.

"We can make our own fun. Thank you very much."

"Oh come on, Susan, you can at least try to be a sport."

"Oh, Janice, you can at least try to be less of a pain in the ass."

"Okay, I'll leave you alone. Whoever wants to play is free to come downstairs and join me in the games room."

"Since when do we have a fucking games room?"

"She means the TV room," I interjected.

"Then why doesn't she just say the fucking TV room?"

"Okay, whatever. I'll go downstairs and wait for you," Janice concluded.

"You can wait until you're fucking blue in the face. I'm not coming down to any fucking games room."

I listened as Janice made her way down the stairs, then I got up.

"Where are you going?" Susan asked.

"Downstairs, to see what it's all about."

"Good for you. I'm not going anywhere."

I met Cindy in the hallway.

"You going down to Janice's thing?" Cindy asked.

I nodded.

"Then let us go together, child," she said in her best fake Jamaican accent as she put her arm around me.

Paula and Janice were the only ones there when we arrived

in the dingy TV room. The puke green walls, ripped couches, and stained rug weren't at all welcoming.

"I'm glad you two decided to join us." Janice was more formal than usual. I could tell she had stepped outside of her comfort zone.

Cindy shook her head as she gawked down at the chessboard on the beat-up coffee table. "Cha," she said rolling her eyes and tapping one of the lawn chairs that Janice had set up.

"Cindy, you and Philomena can be partners and Paula and I can be—"

"How is this going to work?" Paula interrupted.

"Well...I..." Janice started. It was clear she was thinking on her feet. "I thought since it's just the four of us, each pair could play...three games, and then the two winners of those games can play each other three times, and the winner of those games will be the winner."

"That's not going to work. Do you know how long it takes to play a game of chess? Never mind three," Paula interrupted.

"It's not going to work either, because I don't know how to play chess," Cindy added. "Do you know how to play, Philomena?"

I shook my head. No one had ever taught me, and I was never interested in learning.

"You see, she can't play either. It's not something people do in the islands."

"Why didn't you tell me that you couldn't play before?" Janice asked.

"Why didn't you ask?" Cindy snapped.

Janice sighed, looking defeated.

"Now, if you have some checkers, we could do that. Everyone knows how to play checkers," Cindy offered.

"Yeah, checkers, that would work," Paula agreed.

Janice took a second to think. "Yeah, I know where some are. I'll be right back." She jogged out of the room.

149

"That woman is a piece of work. She thinks playing kids games is going to save us," Cindy said.

"People find hope in the strangest ways," Paula replied.

I said nothing. I knew it was guilt and guilt alone that had driven her to do what she was doing.

When Janice returned with the two boxes of checkers, we all smiled and pretended to be thrilled. She rushed to set up the board before we lost interest.

As we played, I moved my men without much thought. Cindy did the opposite. "Bam! Blouse and skirts! Crown me," she yelled when her men reached the last row. The fact that she almost disrupted all the pieces didn't bother her. She got more and more excited with each crown and got up and danced after each of her wins. Janice beat Paula, so Cindy had to face Janice for the final rounds.

As I watched the pair slide their red and black men over the red and black squares, my thoughts went back to the spots of Heike's blood on the asphalt.

"Bam, crown me," Cindy yelled.

"Is that really necessary, Cindy?" Janice asked as she adjusted the pieces on the board and crowned Cindy's man.

"It's the way my brethren play. Right, Philomena?" Cindy replied.

I looked up from the board and nodded even though I had no idea what she had just said.

Chapter 31

SUSAN WAS SITTING on the edge of the bed when I returned to the bedroom. She looked more jittery than usual.

"Are you trying to quit smoking again?" I asked, crawling into bed.

"No, I just finished a pack. Why did you ask me that?"

"Because you don't look right."

"What do you mean I don't look right?"

"Just like I said. What's wrong with you, anyhow?"

"There is nothing wrong with me," she yelled.

"You see."

Susan was silent.

"Why don't you tell yourself a story, Susan?"

"I don't feel like it."

"You see."

"You see what? Why do you keep saying that?"

"Because you're not yourself, Susan Peters."

Susan got up from the bed and started pacing around the room. This, too, was out of character.

"You're absolutely right, Phil. I'm not good. There's something going on inside, and I don't know what it is."

Philomena (Unloved)

"Did they give you different medication?"

"No, I'm taking the same old shit."

"Then what can it be? Is it Heike?"

Her head flopped down and she went back to her bed. "I didn't even know her that well. We'd been in this house together for so many years, and I hardly said boo to her. That's not right, Phil. People should talk to one another. I think that's why they put us together in this room, so we could talk to each other. Everyone else in the house has their own room but us, we share. I think it's a good thing, Phil, having someone to talk to. Having someone to care about if you live or die. Death is an awful thing when you're alone, Phil."

"You're not alone, Susan. You have your family."

"Some family! They can't stand seeing me. You should see it—every time I go over there for a visit, my sister and brother-in-law walk on eggshells trying not to say the wrong thing that might upset me, as if I'm some porcelain doll or something. Do I look like a porcelain doll, Phil? No, I don't think so," she continued without waiting for a reply. "They've treated me like that ever since I was diagnosed. Did I ever tell you that my parents told my sister that I had a tiny penis when I was born, and they cut it off? She told me I was what they call a *hermaphrodite*. Now, do I look like a fucking *hermaphrodite* to you, Phil? Do I look like some sort of freak?"

To avoid a fight, I said nothing.

"You know, I was very beautiful when I was young. Did I ever show you that picture of me, Phil? I was stunning. I could have been a model is what everyone used to say, if only it wasn't for that little penis. I could have been the queen of Sheba if I wanted to. I would have had a king and some princes. I met a guy once who wanted to marry me. He actually proposed and all. We actually set a date, but a day before the wedding, he comes to my house and tells me that he doesn't want to marry me anymore on account of the fact that I can't have kids. He wanted to have a big family, and I couldn't give that to him, so that was it. No one ever asked me again. I guess nobody would want a sterile woman who used to have a penis. I swear, Phil, I wanted to kill someone when I first heard about the prick. I wanted to kill my parents and my sister for telling me, and then I wanted to kill myself, Phil. You hear me, Phil? I wanted to do what that poor Scandinavian girl did. Jump in front of a bus and get my head mashed up and spread all over the highway. But that's no way to die, is it Phil? No way at all. You know, all these years I wanted to ask my mother if what my sister said was true, but I never did. Now my father's dead and the poor old girl is senile—not right in her head. But I think she still knows who I am—at least my sister and her husband say she does. They keep living grand in that house waiting for the poor old girl to croak like the bunch of vultures they are—a pathetic bunch of vultures. You ever see a vulture in a tree, Phil? I saw one on TV once. It just sat there waiting in a tree for the lion to finish killing a gazelle. That's what my sister and her husband and their good-for-nothing little brats are doing. I wish I still had that penis; I would whip it out and piss all over every last one of them. I would. It would be funny, too, because they wouldn't expect it." She giggled. "I would just love to see the look on their faces. It would be better than gold." She pulled the covers over herself. "It would be fucking hilarious…. You want to hear a story, Phil? I feel like telling one now. I feel a little better."

"Good," I said, resting my head back on my pillow. *If that was the truth*, I thought, *it was better than most of her stories.*

"Well, there was this dude who was born with a vagina." She sniggered. "Oh, wait a minute, there was something I wanted to tell you. I keep forgetting to tell you that there is this woman who lives some blocks down the street who reminds me of you every time I see her. I keep seeing her on the way back from my doctor's appointment and visiting my mom. She really reminds me of you. She doesn't really look like you that much; she's taller and more elegant. I don't know what it is exactly about her that reminds me of you, but she just does. Now isn't that strange, Phil?"

"Very," I said, half listening. I was beginning to doze off.

"So, back to the guy with the vagina." Susan snickered.

Chapter 32

AS THE DAY of my departure for America approached, I became more and more convinced that I had made the right decision. Ratina's death and my failed attempt at following her only added fuel to the fire. I hadn't considered my future, or how I could benefit from foreign education. My main motivation was the possibility of seeing my mother. It was a dream I held tight to. The only reason for staying was Pauly, but I sensed that he no longer wanted me there.

A few days before my flight, he presented me with a stylish blue dress. "This is so that you will be presentable for your trip," he said.

It was strange to receive it, since he had never bought me clothes before. I wasn't even quite sure how he had figured out my size. It was a perfect fit, and just the type of dress I would have gotten for myself if I'd had the money.

He held up the dress for me the moment I stepped through the door. I almost burst into tears when I saw it. I knew what the blue fabric symbolized. It was the end—good-bye. It was leaving and possibly never returning. It was the end of longings that could be easily fulfilled. It was the end of him and me and we and us. It was just the end.

155

Philomena (*Unloved*)

"What do you think?" Pauly asked. "You like it?"

I touched it to see how soft it was.

"I got it with long sleeves because those planes are usually cold."

"What does it feel like in the plane, all the way up there?" I asked, just to say something that wasn't remotely confrontational. I had flung all kinds of accusations and bad words at him the last time we'd met, and it had left me feeling guilty.

"It doesn't feel like anything much. It's still—just like we're standing here now. That's how smooth it feels. Mind you, sometimes it does get a bit bumpy, like when you're on a boat and the water is rough, but it only gets like that sometimes. You don't have to worry. Those pilots know what they're doing. I flew to England before and…"

As I watched his face, I noticed certain aspects of it for the very first time. Things I had overlooked before. There was a fine scar just beside his right eye. On his lip, there was a black blotch. A similar one was on his chin. He really wasn't handsome by anyone's definition. His eyes were droopy and his nose too big for his face. The lips were thin and unappealing. His ears had enough hair to compensate for his balding head. The black dye he used only accentuated the gray stubble. I couldn't believe that I had slept with such an ugly man for so long without ever truly seeing him.

"In any case, planes are great inventions. Most importantly, they will allow me to visit you. You don't have to worry about that, Philomena. I will visit you, for sure," he said at the conclusion of his story. What the story had been about was lost on me because I had not heard a single word. His unpleasant face had been too distracting.

"Why don't you try it on," he suggested, holding up the blue dress.

I watched his hands as they clumsily unbuttoned the clasps at the back of the dress. His claws were unsightly. Those same hands had touched me millions of times. They had held my breasts and had been inserted into me. They had held my head straight while I sucked him. They had invaded every part of me without exception and yet I had never really looked at them. They were square and large, stubby and rough. The coarseness had not been something that bothered me as an adult, but as I watched him unfasten the clasp, I felt sorry for those tiny metal hooks. They had done nothing for him to accost them like that.

"Don't pull so hard on them," I heard myself say. "You might break them."

"Oh, we don't want to do that, now do we," he replied, not detecting the disgust in my voice.

With the fasteners undone, he lifted off the dress that I wore and threw it to the ground like a piece of garbage and slipped the new one on me.

"Perfect," he said.

I nodded and stood still as he fumbled to refasten the hooks.

"Never mind, it's okay," I insisted. My concern for the fasteners had grown.

He took this as some sort of cue and undid his belt. A disturbing growl came out of him after his pants were on the floor. I wasn't sure if he had ever made that sound before.

"Come, come, you can take it off now. Let's go to bed," he moaned.

I was in no rush so I took my time. I tied the matching sash around the dress to see how it would look.

"Come, come," he repeated from the bedroom.

I obeyed this time and took off the dress and dropped it next to the old one.

He was already naked by the time I reached him.

His large protruding belly looked as if it was running away from him. He had piled on the pounds over the years. When I got closer, I noticed a scattered pattern of blotches all over his gut similar to the ones on his face. Some of them were raised and had an odd texture to them.

"Come, come. I want you to get on top," he groaned.

I climbed atop him like I had done millions of times before. The stomach that I had once believed to be hard and muscular was now all jelly. I had to use my legs to grip his thighs so that I wouldn't slip. Since his penis was not always ready, it was my job to find it in the mass of fat and help him along. I squirmed at the thought of touching the squishy thing. Once the thrusting began, I hardly felt a thing. The opposite was true for him. His labored breathing and grunts told me that he was either exhilarated or about to lose consciousness. I marvel at the fact that I was normally in the grips of pleasure with him, but this time was different. That day, I was not an active participant. I was someone watching the act from close up. I was in the room, but I was not present. That night, the pastor was screwing a figment of his imagination. A ghost. Something that didn't truly exist. Or maybe it was the opposite. Maybe I hadn't existed before and that night I was more present than I had ever been. Maybe that's why I was noticing things that I had been blind to before.

The sweat halo that formed around the pastor's head when he was done wasn't at all becoming. The musky wetness of his chest and lower regions made me want to vomit. I held my breath as I dismounted and passed him a towel. I stayed to watch as his whole body shook when he wiped himself dry.

"I'm going to go and wash myself," he announced as he got up and hung the towel around his neck.

His flat, hairy backside was just as repulsive as his front. I prayed that he would have the good sense to put on his robe when he got out of the shower.

"Are you okay today?" he asked as he nudged my leg. I had dozed off while he showered.

"Don't you want to shower?"

I shook my head emphatically, even though I was dying to wash his musk off of me.

"Why are you acting so strange?"

"I don't know," I replied, telling the truth.

"You know, you're really not going all that far. There is really no need to worry your pretty head about any of it. If you need anything, whatever it may be, all you have to do is write me and it'll be yours. Imagine, when you're done, you'll be better educated than all those nurses in our main hospital put together."

I nodded, even though I had not given school a second thought. I had considered the distance and strangeness many times, but my biggest worry, outside of not being able to find my mother, was the cold. I had gone into Mrs. Payne's shop one day and asked if I could stick my head in her deep freeze to see what the cold felt like, but she just shooed me away. I had to, instead, go to the capital to a shop where I didn't know the owner. I wasn't able to get the full effect of the backroom freezer before a woman in an old housecoat found me. "Get your ass out of there before I call the police. Something wrong with your head, sticking your face in my deep freeze?" She continued yelling as I ran out of the store. "You better go to the doctor and get yourself checked out."

As I stood there staring at the pastor in his white robe, I wondered if that woman in the capital had been right. Maybe there was something wrong with my head.

"Will you really visit me?" I asked, catching myself.

He gave me a strange look. I could tell that he was thrown off by my odd behavior.

"Of course I will. If I tell you I'm going to do something, I'll do it. Have I ever made a promise to you that I didn't keep?"

He was right. He had always done whatever he said he would do. He would arrive close to the time he said he would arrive. He would bring me the sweets that he'd promised. He had promised to pay for my school uniforms and books and had done that. Ratina hadn't approved of what was going on between us, but she recognized the economic benefits.

"If you choose to lie with that old, fat pig of a man," Ratina had said, forgetting that he was by then the pastor of her church, "then you are beyond repair, my child. I am just sorry for you."

Ratina and the woman in the capital were both right. There was something terribly not right with me. I didn't fully understand this until many years later—long after my good-bye to the pastor and long after the wheels of the plane touched down in my new home.

Chapter 33

CINDY WAS ALWAYS asking me to go places with her; to this or that friend or this or that party or event. She knew a lot of people. The majority of them were Caribbean. For this reason, she assumed I would feel right at home.

"And you could eat some nice rice and peas and chicken like back home," she would say to entice me. But I was never interested in meeting any of her friends or going to any of her parties. I preferred to stay at home alone in the room, or with Susan. Susan was just about enough company for me.

When Cindy entered our room one morning dressed in a plain beige summer dress with her hair down, carrying a medium-sized duffle bag, I knew right away that something was amiss. The only time I had seen her in plain colors without a head wrap was at Heike's funeral. I could tell that she was on her way to somewhere somber.

"Where are you going? You not leaving us, are you?" Susan asked in the middle of a puff.

"No, I'm going…I'm going to see my kid."

Susan choked on the inhale. "You have a kid? Why didn't I know about this?"

"Yes, I have a kid…a daughter. She's living with my mother now."

"Where was she before?"

"Where do you think?"

"Foster care."

"That poor kid. Some of those foster places are horrible, I hear."

"Yeah, I know all about them," Cindy replied. "They wouldn't let me see her when she was there, but now that she's with my mom, it's different."

"How old is she?" Susan asked. She was as nosey as any of the old ladies back home. "Sixteen."

"How old was she when you saw her last?" I asked.

"Two," she answered matter-of-factly, but I could see the turmoil in her eyes.

"Two! My God. You missed out on her whole life." Susan sat up in bed. She looked as if she was getting ready to ask more questions.

"Tell me something I don't know, Susan Peters," Cindy replied, mimicking the way I handled Susan. "Philomena, I wanted to ask if you would come along with me. I'm kind of nervous. Will you come with me, please? I think I'd feel better if I had someone with me."

"What's in the bag?" Susan asked.

"None of your business."

I had never seen Cindy look so distraught, so I decided to go.

"How far is it?"

"Don't worry, I'll pay your carfare if that's what you're worried about."

"No, I just wanted to know how long it would take to get there."

"Oh, at least an hour or so. My mother lives out in the boonies."

I slid out of bed.

Cindy flashed a smile. I could tell she was relieved that I was going with her.

Our ride on the bus, the subway, and the second bus was quiet. I preferred it like that. It gave me an opportunity to take in the city that I had lived in for some years but didn't really know. As we got farther away from the downtown core, I felt myself relaxing as the roads became wider and buildings farther apart. I appreciated the space. It reminded me of home. The sky was not as blue and the vegetation not as lush, but the airiness was similar.

Cindy spent most of the trip staring at her feet or the bag, looking only occasionally out the window to see where we were. Her body seemed to get more rigid as the trip went along. When we reached our stop and stepped down from the bus, Cindy placed the bag on the ground and pointed to a house at the end of the block. The cluster of townhouses was identically bland.

"That's the house," she announced with dread. "Can you believe that's subsidized housing? I wish I could have grown up out here, but she only got this place a few years ago on account of her disability."

I could tell that she was just stalling, trying to postpone the inevitable. She stood there and babbled for a good five minutes as cars and people moved by us.

"Shouldn't we go?" I finally asked.

"Yeah, let's bite the bullet." She took a deep breath, picked up the bag, and led the way.

Cindy's mother was standing in front of the house waiting for us. She must have seen us when we got off the bus. She looked more like Cindy's sister than her mother. As I watched them greet each other with a hardy bear hug, I wondered what the mother's disability was. There was nothing obvious in her appearance.

"Oh Cindy, Cindy, Cindy. My Cindy Lou," she chanted.

"Ma, how are you?"

"I'm as good as I can get," Cindy's mother said with a chuckle. "Come in, please, come in."

"Ma, this is my friend Philomena. She lives where I live."

Cindy's mother nodded at me. "Good to know you, Philomena. Please come in."

I wanted to shake her hand but she turned around too quickly. I followed the large matching rumps into the house. When Cindy froze, I knew that she had seen her daughter. I peered over her shoulder to see an adolescent version of Cindy sitting passively on the living-room couch. The mop of curly hair on her head and her darker skin tone was the only marked difference. They were clearly mother and child.

"Cher, this is your mother. Cindy…Cher."

The bag fell out of Cindy's hand. This made Cher flinch.

I couldn't see Cindy's face, but I knew she was crying. She started to quake and then slumped over. This is when I could finally hear the sobs.

Cher fidgeted with her fingers for a second, then got up and walked over to her mother. She stood at arm's length from her and gently touched her shoulder. Cindy looked up at her and cried even louder. Cindy's mother facilitated the reunion by softly nudging the pair closer together. They immediately fell into a deep embrace. By this time Cindy was inconsolable.

"Sorry…sorry…sorry," Cindy wailed.

As I stood there watching the momentous event, I couldn't help but wonder how I would react if I were reunited with my mother. Tears rolled down my face at the thought of it. Even more came as I felt the anguish of both Cindy and her daughter.

"Well, why don't we all go and get some cake," Cindy's

mother insisted. "Cher and I made it this morning. It took a lot out of me not to cut it after we finished icing it. Cher knows I have very little willpower."

Cher wiped away the solitary tear from her eye and smiled. There was something reserved about her demeanor.

"Come, let's wash the tears down with some milk." Cindy's mother started walking toward the back of the house.

"Wait, I have something for Cher." Cindy took a step back and unzipped the bag she'd brought. "I got you some new jeans and shirts and stuff, but I also saved something for you from when you were small, before they…before I…when you were still living with me."

Cindy pulled a plush blue dog out of the bag and showed it to Cher.

"I bought this for you on your first birthday. I kept it because I thought you might want it someday."

Cindy handed the toy to her daughter, and her daughter held it by its head, not knowing what to do with it. She shuffled uncomfortably without saying a word.

"All right, that's enough of that for now. It's cake time."

I stood still and watched as Cindy and Cher followed Cindy's mother into the kitchen. Realizing that I wasn't behind her, Cindy turned.

"Come on, Philomena, my mother meant you too."

I followed.

In the kitchen, everyone sat and watched silently as Cindy's mother cut four pieces of cake and placed them carefully onto small floral plates.

"It's pecan flavor, your favorite, Cindy," she announced as she handed one plate to each of us.

No words were spoken as we picked at the cake. The lumps in our throats left little room for swallowing.

Cindy stared at her daughter, and her daughter stared at her plate.

Philomena *(Unloved)*

"So how is school and all that stuff?" Cindy asked, breaking the silence.

"It's good. I'm doing much better now, since I've been here with Nana."

"That's good. That's good to hear."

As the four of us sat there awkwardly for the next half hour, I listened while Cindy and her daughter exchanged words like strangers meeting for the first time. The words were stiff and lacked the emotion that was displayed earlier.

I turned my body sideways and fixed my eyes on the window that faced the backyard so it wouldn't seem like I was eavesdropping.

"I'm going to go outside for a bit, if that's okay," I announced as I got up and headed toward the back door. Since no one answered, I assumed that I wasn't offending anyone.

"Why don't you two go back and sit in the living room," I heard Cindy's mother say as I closed the door behind me.

The backyard was small but functional. I sat down in the swinging seat that had a canopy over it. It was the only place with any trace of shade. I didn't like sitting in the sun.

"We're black enough. We don't need to sunbathe like those foreigners," Ratina had always said.

While the chair rocked gently back and forth, I looked at the row of identical backyards and disappeared once again into thoughts of my mother. I wondered if she had been lucky enough to get a subsidized townhouse like this one in the suburbs. If so, I wondered if the house made her happy and if the yard made her long for the vastness of Ratina's property back home. I wondered if she ever thought about me or prayed for our reunion like I did. I wondered if our reunion would be as emotional and awkward as Cindy and her daughter's. Would we also be like strangers? In that moment, I realized that Cher and I would have been about the same age when we were separated from our mothers. Both of us had spent the same number of sunny mornings and rainy nights with our mothers. For both of us, that separation would have been damaging to our emotional well-being. I wondered if Cher had a person like the pastor in her life. If so, did she long for him the way I had longed for the pastor? All these thoughts exploded in my head simultaneously, giving me a headache. When I closed my eyes, I was lulled to sleep by the back and forth motion of the swinging chair.

My mother appeared to me in my dream, or at least I felt it was her, since I no longer remembered what she looked like. She was a petite woman with large, soulful eyes. She came up to me and attempted to pick me up as if I were still a child. Since I was fully grown, her attempts were fruitless.

"How is my little baby girl?" she said, touching my cheek.

"I'm not your little girl," I replied.

"You'll always be my little sweet one."

"I'm not little or sweet," I insisted. I wiped off the spot where she touched me. "Where the hell have you been all this time?" I demanded.

"I've been right here with you all the time. I never left."

"You're a fucking liar. You left me a long time ago. You were never fucking here. You have no idea what I had to go through all because you left me, you fucking, selfish bitch."

"Well if you're going to be so rude and call me names, maybe I should just leave."

"Maybe you should, you fucking bitch."

"Okay, good-bye," she said as she took a few steps toward me, attempting to kiss me on my forehead.

I moved so that she couldn't reach me.

"Okay, you want to be like that, I'm going to leave. Bye, Philomena," she said and then disappeared.

I panicked. I didn't want to lose her again. "No, I changed my mind. Please come back. Ma, Ma…Ma."

"Philomena!" Cindy yelled as she shoved my shoulder. "Wake up, nah."

Her distressed face greeted me when I opened my eyes. She held the duffle bag in her hand.

"Let's get out of here," she said emphatically.

"Already? We just got here." I had enjoyed the quiet of the suburbs even though it had brought back thoughts of my mother.

"Yeah, already. They don't want me here."

"What happened?"

"Never mind. Let's just go catch the fucking bus."

I followed behind her without any further questions.

On the long ride back, Cindy's pain was palpable. She stared at the back of the seat in front of her and held on to the bag as if her life depended on it. I could tell she regretted ever making the trip. It appeared that it had done more harm than good.

In the subway, Cindy stared into the blackness outside the window, then to the floor when we reached each stop. The ride was doing little to calm her feelings.

When we were just outside the rooming house, Cindy turned around and looked at me for the first time since the suburbs.

"You know what she said to me?"

I gave her the most comforting look I could. I knew that my words were not necessary.

"She said that I ruined her life."

I thought if I had the opportunity, I would have said the same thing to my mother.

"She told me that she wished I had just given her up when she was born. She said she might have had a better chance, and that she wouldn't have ended up with the psycho foster families she'd been placed with. She showed me the spot on her leg where she cut herself and all the scars she'd got from being beaten to a pulp. I told her I was sorry, and I asked her to forgive me, but she said it was too late. My mother pleaded with her, too, but she refused. And look—"

Cindy opened the bag and pulled out the blue dog.

"I asked her to keep it even if she didn't want the clothes, but she just said, 'I don't want your fucking clothes or the fucking dog.' She told me that I could 'shove it up my fucking ass.' I guess I deserve it after all I put her through. I could have prevented all of it if I'd been a better mother, if I'd fought to keep her, if I hadn't been so stupid and selfish." She began to sob.

"We can only do what we know," I told her, repeating something Ratina had often said.

"Well, I should have known better."

"You did a good thing today by going to visit her and trying to make amends. It takes a strong person to face their mistakes," I offered. I put my hand on Cindy's shoulder, knowing that no amount of words or support could provide her with the comfort or peace that she needed.

Chapter 34

THE APARTMENT THAT the pastor had secured for me was in a busy part of town. I felt as if I had arrived in outer space with the tall buildings that reached up into the sky like rockets and the cars that rushed by with lightning speed. I almost got run over a few times. All the new things were so distracting, I could barely pay attention to where I was going.

The first thing I did, before unpacking or looking for something to eat, was find a phone book. Luckily there were a few of them left behind in the furnished apartment. The phone was still connected, so I took advantage of it. I was determined to find my mother, wherever she was. I sat and diligently called all the Donna Joneses that were listed in the white pages. (She had not taken my father's last name even though his family had insisted.) Each time I asked, "Can I please speak to Donna Jones?" And each time I held my breath in anxious anticipation.

"This is she," the first voice answered with an English accent. Knowing it wasn't my mother, I hung up immediately. None of the voices had a cadence that resembled mine. The closest I got was a woman from Jamaica. When she started cursing me out for calling her in the middle of the night—it was 11:15

p.m.—and waking up her children, I knew that I had failed again.

Having no luck with the Donna Joneses, I then moved on to the D. Joneses. This was even more fruitless. I had no idea if she was even in this same city where I was. I didn't give up there, though. When I found out that the library had phone books for every city in the country, I decided that I would try as many Donna Joneses as I could afford to call. This didn't amount to very many.

"Yes, hello. I'm looking for Donna Jones."

"Yes, she lives here," someone replied with an accent I didn't recognize. "One moment please."

I took a deep breath.

"Yes, what can I do for you?" that Donna Jones said in an indistinguishable accent. I hung up. I still had not found my Donna Jones. She was the tiniest of needles, and the country was a vast haystack.

Eventually I gave up the hope of ever finding my mother. I felt as if I had lost her yet again. Hope, I had learned, was one of God's cruelest inventions.

Chapter 35

I SETTLED INTO school immediately. My classes were interesting and my classmates friendly. The teachers were well prepared and less formal than they were back home. The transition was smoother than I had anticipated. All the young men I approached were more than willing to please me. None of them cared when I moved on to the next. After a while, I didn't even bother learning their names. I followed strict rules to keep myself safe and out of danger. I never brought anyone home. I always used protection. And I only chose Black men. I also kept my distance because I didn't want a repeat of what had happened with Trevor years earlier.

What I had not properly prepared myself for, however, was the weather. The few stolen minutes in that woman's deep freeze had not been sufficient. It seemed as if the temperature got progressively colder each day as the weeks and months went by. I kept on thinking that it couldn't possibility get any colder, then Mother Nature proved me wrong. I bolstered my fight with her by adding layers on top of layers. It was close to the end of October when a classmate of mine said, "You should really get yourself a winter jacket." I agreed with her and went that same day to the secondhand store and found one. It made

Christene A. Browne

all the difference in the world. But just when I was starting to feel more at ease in my new home, October 31 arrived. It was a Saturday evening.

First, I heard all kinds of scurrying in the hallways. It sounded as if the children's playground had been moved indoors. I wanted to open the door to see what all the noise was about, but I didn't bother. However, when there was an assault of tiny knuckles on my door, I was forced to look. In front of me was a group of children, all of them wearing sheets over their heads with slits cut into them for their noses and eyes. And each of them held open a plastic bag.

"Trick or treat," they all yelled in unison.

My first thought was that I was having some sort of hallucination similar to the voices that I had been hearing, but then I noticed a couple, the parents I assumed, standing behind the kids smiling. *People don't smile in hallucinations*, I thought.

"Trick or treat," the children repeated.

"I'm sorry, I don't understand," I said, directing my statement to the adults.

"The kids are trick-or-treating for Halloween," the mother answered.

"What's that? I'm not from here."

"Oh, oh sorry," the mother said giggling. "This must seem really strange for you then. Are you from the Caribbean? I went to St. Martin once to do missionary work. It was beautiful."

"Yes, I'm from the Caribbean," I answered, looking at the parade of kids and parents running up and down the hall.

"But you're not from St. Martin, are you?"

"How do you know?"

"Your accent."

"Oh," I said, feeling somewhat exposed.

"So, the kids dress up in costume and knock on the doors, and people are supposed to give out candy when the kids say 'trick or treat,'" the father interrupted.

Philomena *(Unloved)*

"And money too!" The smallest ghost pulled out an orange tin box from under his sheet.

"Yes, some kids collect money for UNICEF too," the father continued.

"Well, I don't have any sweets, but I can give you some change. Is that all right?" I asked, fearful that the tiny ghost would come back to haunt me.

"That's fine. That's okay. It's better than candy. It doesn't cause cavities," the mother added.

"Nothing is better than candy," the large ghost said, heading off to the next door.

I ran to get my purse and emptied all of my loose change into the orange box.

"Now I'm going to have more money than everyone else," the smallest ghost said excitedly.

"The money is not for you. It's for poor kids, Jack," his mother reminded him.

"I could take some and give the rest to the poor kids. We're poor too, aren't we, Mom?"

The mother was too embarrassed to speak.

"Just thank the lady, Jack, and let's go," the father ordered.

"Thank you."

When they were gone, I closed the door, turned my lights off, and pretended that nobody was home. I had nothing more to offer.

As I listened to the ruckus, I tiptoed to the window to get a look at what was happening outside. The scene from the hallway was mirrored out there. Little and big creatures scurried about as tiny white particles whirled around them. I wondered first if the white dust was part of this strange ritual, but then I realized it wasn't. The quantity and the way it danced about in the sky and disappeared like magic when it reached the ground told me that it was something only Mother Nature could create. Wanting to experience it, I opened the window and removed the screen.

174

The flakes felt wet and cold as they landed in my palm. I kept my hand out there for as long as I could until it got too cold. The revelers vanished, and I spent the next hours taking in the wonder of my first snowfall.

❧

I saw Ratina in my dream that night and got very worried. She had told me that when someone dreams of a dead person, it means that a death has occurred or one is coming.

I tried not to think about death the next day during the biology test. When we exchanged papers, I noticed the person whose work I had corrected had not done well.

"You should study a little harder," I offered as I handed the test back.

"You got perfect again!" the girl in front of me cheered. "She got perfect again, Mr. Sinclair."

This news made me happy and helped me temporarily forget about death and dreams.

I decided to celebrate my test results by treating myself to a store-bought lunch rather than my usual sardines and bread. "Pizza," I said to myself. "I think I'll buy myself some pizza."

At the food court in the complex a few blocks away, I purchased the cheapest slice and found a seat. Just as I was about to take my first bite, someone tugged my arm. I turned around and looked up at a face that seemed more foreign than familiar to me. His smooth brown skin looked out of place.

"You don't know me now?" the pudgy young man smirked.

My mouth was wide open.

"Albert? Is that you, Albert?"

Albert Morris had been my classmate from the time I started school. He had even helped me one time with a letter I wrote to my mother. He had never gone to the bushes with me, but I heard he had wanted to.

Philomena (Unloved)

"Oh, now you know me. I was waiting to see if I could catch your eye, but you walked right by me."

"What are you doing here, Albert?"

"The same as you."

"How long have you been here? When did you come?" I was stunned to see someone from my former life.

"Not too long ago."

I got up to embrace him.

"Well how is everything and everyone back home?" By everyone I meant the pastor. I knew he would know who I was talking about since they were neighbors.

"You don't know? You haven't heard yet?"

"Heard what?"

"The pastor died two weeks ago."

"What?" I yelled at the top of my lungs. I felt my knees buckle beneath me as hundreds of eyes stared at me.

Albert had to grab my arm to prevent me from falling.

"Are you sure?" I asked, holding my chest. My heart felt as if it would erupt. I had just received a letter from him the week before.

"Yes, I'm more than sure."

"Who told you?"

"My cousin."

"How?"

"What do you mean how?"

"How? How did it happen? How did he die?"

"They said it was his heart," he lied. I found out later that the pastor had been beaten by the father of a young girl.

"Did he suffer much?" I asked.

"No, he said it was pretty instant," he lied again. The father had broken the pastor's jaw and a few of his ribs, but it was a lingering post-surgical infection that killed him. He spent his last days alone in the hospital clinging to life. His wife had refused his many pleas to join him in his final hours.

"Good. That's good. I'm so glad he didn't suffer," I said, trying to compose myself.

"So, do you live in the area?" Albert asked, trying to ease some of the tension.

"Not very far from here," I answered, wiping my face.

"Well it's a shame that we are just meeting now. I'm about to move out west. They say there's more work in that part of the country. I think maybe I might try construction, and if that doesn't work, I guess I can do some cleaning until I'm able to find something better."

"Oh," I replied half listening. "I think it's time for me to get back to class," I added in a daze. I patted Albert on the shoulder and gave him half a hug.

"Are you sure you're okay?" Albert asked.

"I'm fine. Just fine," I answered without bothering to look back.

With the slice of pizza in my hand, I walked out of the food court.

One of my classmates standing outside said something to me, but I heard nothing.

"Did something happen to you?" she said louder.

I shook my head, turned around, and handed her the pizza. She gave me a strange look.

I walked mechanically into the classroom and sat down. *How am I going to survive without the pastor?* I thought. *How will I live without his help? How am I going to eat and pay my rent?* The school fees had been paid for the year, but after that, what was I going to do? I felt heartbroken, confused, angry, and doomed all at once.

"Is anything wrong, Philomena?" the teacher asked.

"No, nothing's wrong," I lied.

In the days that followed, the impact of the pastor's death set in. I walked about in a zombie-like state, paying attention to nothing and no one. I didn't eat and only slept when I could

Philomena (Unloved)

no longer keep my eyes open. I couldn't find the will to leave my apartment, not even to go to school. There was a heavy gravitational force that kept me planted and pulled me back each time I made an attempt to move.

I wanted to scream, *Look what you've done. Look what you did to the only man I ever loved. Look what you did to him. Now he's gone.* I wanted to find someone, anyone, to blame, but I couldn't find anyone, so I blamed myself. This only made things worse.

I lay in bed unbathed, starving myself, only getting up to use the toilet and drink rusty water from the bathroom sink. I thought of the last time I saw him, the disgust I felt, and the feelings of regret that washed over me the second the plane had landed. I wanted to fly back and apologize for my coldness and my distance and my unexplained repulsion. I wanted to lie in his arms and enjoy his company. I only found solace after I received his first letter. The tone of it told me that I had been forgiven. This had eased my mind but I still filled my reply with words of love, admiration, and gratitude. I wanted him to know that I still loved him.

After a few weeks of wallowing in grief and regret, I had had enough. I woke up one morning, saw the sun, and got out of bed. There was a sudden glimmer of inexplicable hope. I didn't know where it came from or what had triggered it, but I was grateful for it. I was able to clear the negative thoughts from my mind, defy their pull, and finally get back to living.

On the way to school that morning, I absentmindedly walked into the broad chest of a young man. It was only after I stepped back from him that I noticed he looked like a younger version of the pastor, or that is what my grieving mind told me.

"I'm so sorry," the man said. "I wasn't looking where I was

going." He was dressed in a smart navy suit, the same shade of blue the pastor often wore.

"Me neither," I confessed.

"Are you okay? You're not hurt?"

"No, I'm fine." I stared at the man's face. The more I stared at him, the more he looked like the pastor.

"Good, good. I'm glad you're okay. Take care." He hurried off.

I felt compelled to follow him, but I didn't.

The next day I saw the same man again. This time he was closer to the school, and he greeted me with a guilty grin and a nod.

These chance meetings continued for several weeks and came to be the highlight of my day.

I would look forward to seeing the tips of the young man's fingers as he waved to me and the plump part of his neck as he walked away. My weekends were spent tidying my apartment, shopping for groceries, and anxiously waiting for Monday to roll around so that I would have a chance to see him again. His presence was exactly what I needed to break up the monotony that had become my life. My existence at the time consisted of school, home, homework, chores, and back to school again. Socializing with the other students and engaging in casual sex were no longer of any interest to me. Most nights when I finished eating and had done my school work, I would end up in bed at seven o'clock, with nothing else to do. The life of a prisoner would have been much more stimulating.

The one thing I did enjoy, however, were my trips to the market. The cluster of shops owned by immigrants, and located only a short streetcar ride away, was where I could find plantain and eddo and fresh fish and all the things I had eaten back home.

One particular Saturday afternoon, as I stepped onto a crowded streetcar, I got the shock of my life when I saw my young man. He was dressed casually. He was looking in the other

Philomena *(Unloved)*

direction as I made my way through the crowd toward him. The closer I got, the more anxious I became. I knew I wanted to say something but I didn't know what.

I touched him on his shoulder, and he turned around. I could tell that I'd surprised him from the awkward look on his face. The smile of recognition that followed put me at ease.

"Fancy meeting you here," he said as if he had known me from birth. "Where are you off to today," he added, forgetting that this was our very first conversation.

"The Jewish market," I stammered in almost a whisper, remembering that Ratina had told me to never talk my business in public.

"Oh. I go there sometimes," he said as he moved out of the way to let someone by. When he moved back, we were forced to stand with our faces inches apart. It was a bit unsettling. "You can't beat their prices."

I nodded.

"And everything's always so fresh," he added.

I looked at him as if I didn't understand English.

"So, you're a student?" he asked

I nodded again.

"What are you studying, if you don't mind my asking?"

I could tell that he sensed my discomfort.

"Nursing," I replied, finally getting hold of my tongue.

"What was that?"

"Nursing," I repeated.

"Nursing, that's great."

There was an uncomfortable pause.

"I work in an insurance company." He swung his head around to look out the window. "Oh, I have to get off."

"Okay," I sighed, wishing that he could stay.

"Do you think I could…? Do you think it would possible for me to get your phone number?" he asked, looking at my shoulder for some reason.

180

"Sure," I said, trying to hide my excitement. The inflection of my voice, however, gave it away. The elation quickly shifted to devastation when I realized that I had nothing to write with. It returned again when he pulled a pen out of his jacket pocket.

"What is it? Go ahead."

I made sure not to say it too loud. I watched as he wrote the number carefully on the palm of his hand.

"Thanks. This is great. So, I'll call you. Have a nice time at the market," he said before slipping out the back door.

As I waved good-bye, I wanted to rush out behind him, but I refrained.

That day I didn't linger at the market as I usually did. I just grabbed what I needed and hurried home. I cooked myself a simple meal, took a quick shower, dressed in my nightgown, and sat by the phone and waited. I stayed in that same position until midnight. The phone never rang.

I had no intention of budging from my bed on Sunday morning, but when the phone rang, I ran to answer it.

"Hello, is this the nursing student?" It was him.

"Yes, it's me," I answered, trying to catch my breath.

"Sorry, I forgot to ask you your name," he continued. "So silly."

"I'm Philomena. And you?"

"It's Lionel. Lionel Thomas. Philomena? I never knew anyone called that before. It's…very pretty."

A long paused followed.

"Sorry, I'm a little nervous," he admitted.

"Me too," I confessed.

"Look…do you like walking?"

"Sure."

"That's great, me too. Would you like to go for a walk today?"

We made arrangements to meet in an hour.

I ate, showered, and dressed in haste and arrived at the

location early. He was already there seated tranquilly on a bench. He greeted me with a bright smile. I smiled back feeling as if all the air had just been knocked out of me.

"I thought I was early," I panted.

"Me too," he said as he stood up and held his hand out to me. "Good to see you."

"Good to see you too."

"Should we walk?" he proposed.

The street was quiet, not many people.

As I walked next to him down the street, I realized that this was the first time I had ever walked with a man in public. It was liberating.

We strolled silently for several blocks, then he dashed into a corner store without any warning. I found it very odd.

"Lionel?"

He returned with two oranges.

"Would you like some?" he asked.

I nodded.

Something about the way he peeled the orange reminded me of home.

I smiled when he handed me half.

"Where are you from?" I asked curiously.

"I was born in France, but my family is from Guadeloupe."

"You don't have an accent."

"I was very young when we came here."

"Oh," I said, not knowing what else to say.

"Should we go up there?" he asked, pointing to a small park on top of a hill.

I was happy to go anywhere with him.

The park consisted of nothing more than a single bench and a patch of grass. It wasn't much to look at, but it was tucked away so that we could have some privacy.

Lionel dusted off the bench with an old newspaper and made

a gentlemanly gesture prompting me to sit.

He surveyed the area before taking a seat himself. I wondered what he was looking for.

"Sir Albert Frontenac III Park," he read the sign directly in front of us. "Such a big name for a small place."

We giggled like two small children.

"Would you like some more?" He fumbled in his pocket and took out the other orange.

"No, thanks," I replied. Citrus fruits were far from my favorite.

He returned it to his pocket, then started looking around as if he had lost something.

"Is everything okay?" I asked.

"Everything is good," he stammered.

"Are you sure?"

"Well, I just wanted to ask you something." He twitched.

"Go ahead."

"Can I…? Would it be okay if I…? I mean, if you didn't want me to I would understand…"

"What was it that you wanted to do?" I wasn't accustomed to this kind of insecurity. The pastor had always been so forceful.

"Do you mind if I touch you?" he finally asked. His tensed shoulders relaxed the second the words were out of his mouth.

"Touch me where?" I asked coyly.

"No, no, not like that," he replied embarrassed. "I just wanted to touch your skin. To see what it feels like."

"My skin?"

"Yeah, I've never touched a Black woman's skin before. I mean, I have, but not like that."

"You mean you've never been with a Black woman before?"

"No, never," he admitted. He didn't seem to be too proud of this admission.

I was stunned.

"So, is it okay then? Can I?"

I nodded my permission and watched as the man who suddenly felt like more of a stranger than before closed his eyes and extended his fingers toward my bare arm. A look of pleasure flooded his face as he stroked me like I was a cat. It felt very odd.

"So soft," he cooed.

"It's the lotion," I replied, looking away.

He didn't seem to notice my uneasiness.

In the weeks that followed, Lionel Thomas had many more opportunities to caress the supple skin of my arm. Our meetings were, for some reason, always outdoors. After several weeks of this, I needed to find out why.

"You sure like these parks, don't you? I asked as I stroked his neck, the only part of his body other than his hand and face that I was familiar with.

"Yeah, why not? They're nice." He slipped his arm around me.

"I think we've been to almost every little park in the city by now."

"What, you don't like them? I thought you liked them."

"No, no, I didn't say that."

"Then what did you mean?" He sounded defensive.

"I just meant that we spend a lot of time in parks. That's all. We never seem to go anywhere else or do anything else."

"We could do something else, if you'd like. What do you want to do?"

"Why don't you ever invite me over to your place, for example?"

"My place? Well…ah…I don't think that would be a good idea," he stuttered and withdrew his arm.

"What's wrong with your place?" I was becoming suspicious, even though clandestine relationships were all I knew.

"Nothing is wrong with my place. It's just that—"

"Just that what? Oh, I see. I should have known."

"You should have known what?"

"That you're married."

"Married? No, I'm not married," he insisted.

"Then why do we always end up in parks? Why can't we go to your place?"

"I thought you liked being outside."

"Well, it's getting rather cold."

"Okay, okay. Next time we'll go to my place then. Would that make you happy?"

"Sure," I said, forcing a smile.

The following Sunday, I was treated to a delicious home-cooked meal in Lionel's tiny bachelor apartment. If he had a wife, there was no place to hide her. The bed was the first thing I noticed when I entered. My attention kept going back to it as we ate.

After dessert, I began to feel moist between my legs—the same way I used to feel when the pastor touched me in certain places. It could have been the wine or the fact that it had been months since I'd last had sex. Whatever it was, I welcomed the sensation.

I walked over to Lionel and brushed the back of my hand against the fresh stubble on his chin. Then, without warning, I reached deep down into his pants.

"What the hell are you doing?" He jumped up and yanked my hands away from him.

That wasn't the reaction I had anticipated.

"I just wanted to get a little close," I moaned.

"I think you were close enough," he shouted, stepping even farther away.

"Why are you yelling? What did I do wrong?"

"You know exactly what you did."

"I thought you would like it."

"Well I didn't like it."

Philomena *(Unloved)*

"I was just trying to start things." I stepped toward him and reached out to touch him.

"I said no." He deflected my arm.

I was dumbfounded.

"Can you please leave now," he ordered.

"You want me to leave?"

"Yes, I want you to go. You should go."

"But?" My advances had never been rejected before. I wasn't quite sure how to feel about it.

"Just leave, please."

As I grabbed my purse, I watched how Lionel stood shaking with his hands over his crotch. I understood then why we spent so much time in public places, why I had never been invited to his place before, and, most importantly, why I had been thrown out. When I groped around in his pants there had been no reaction. His dick was as lifeless as a slab of liver.

Chapter 36

IN THE WEEKS that followed, neither Lionel nor I bothered to communicate. He, I assumed, was too embarrassed. I was indifferent. I spent most of my time locked away in my apartment wallowing in my loneliness. The pastor was dead, Ratina gone, and my mother nowhere to be found. The realization brought my melancholia to the surface and made me feel both burdened and liberated at the same time. Burdened by the sadness, liberated by the knowledge that things would always be the same. Ratina used to say, "No situation is permanent," but she was wrong. My suffering was permanent. I was always in a state of misery. It followed me and was my constant companion. Recognizing this, I woke up one Sunday morning and decided that I would try to do something to shake off that misery that clung to me. I got up and began to jump and shake as if an invisible band were playing the loudest, most dissonant, wildest music ever composed. My jerky motions matched perfectly the music in my head. The louder it got, the more exaggerated my movements became. At the height of my performance, I jumped around the whole apartment, flinging my limbs into the air while I smashed into anything that got in the way. Then the tears came. The more vigorous and joyous the movement, the more abundant the flow. Through blurred vision, I danced on. I stopped only when exhaustion took over. My mood was lifted but my body ached. As I lay there in the middle of the mess that I had created, wiping my tears and trying to catch my breath, there was a knock at the door.

"Philomena, it's me, Lionel," the voice outside the door said.

I didn't budge.

Lionel had never been to my place before so I wondered how he had found me.

"Your friend Shelly from your class told me where you lived," he said, as if reading my thoughts. "Please let me in, Philomena. I know we didn't leave things on very good terms the last time we saw each other."

Everything in me wanted to ignore him, but I forced myself toward the door. I wiped my face quickly with my sleeve before opening the door.

"Sorry for coming here like this."

I could tell that he was surprised by my rumpled appearance.

"Can I come in?"

He stepped in as I opened the door wider.

"I guess, I should say…" he started, pretending not to see the mess in my apartment.

I made an attempt to cover my uncombed hair.

"I just wanted to say…I just wanted to apologize…" He remained standing since the couch was covered in clothes. "I just wanted to tell you what I should have told you before… about…" He was struggling with his words.

"About your limp dick," I said, staring at my dirty floor.

"Yes," he said, swallowing nervously. Had I been a good host, I would have offered him some water, but there wasn't a clean glass in the whole place.

"That was the reason I didn't want you coming to my apartment in the first place, so that I could avoid exactly what happened. I know I could have told you, but I was just too embarrassed, and I then I thought, with you there, maybe I would get some movement...you know...get aroused, but it didn't happen, so I just wanted to say that I was sorry."

"No need to apologize," I said with my head still down.

"I at least owe you that."

"You owe me nothing."

"Yes, yes, I owe you an explanation, at least."

"No, you don't."

"Yes, I do."

We were at a stalemate. The words were circling around me and making me dizzy.

"Are you all right?" he asked, concerned.

I looked up as his words sailed out of his mouth toward the ceiling.

"I think you should go," I heard myself say. I really wanted him to stay and hold me and take care of me and kiss me tenderly on the forehead as the pastor and my mother once did, but I couldn't say those things. It was too difficult to express.

He stepped toward me.

"I can't go just yet. I still haven't told you what I came to tell you."

"It doesn't matter what you have to say. It doesn't change anything," I said, looking directly at him for the first time.

"If you let me say it, it might."

"No, I don't want to hear it. I think you should go and leave me alone. I'm better like this."

"No one is better alone, Philomena."

"I am."

"Well, don't you want to hear what I came to tell you? I want to make things better for you and me."

"You and me," I mocked. "There is no you and me. There is only me and me. Do you understand, it's just me and my lonesome."

"It doesn't have to be that way, Philomena. I could—"

"Please go," I heard myself say.

"But...I—"

"Go," I said, closing my eyes and pointing to the door.

He left without another word.

The next day he called, and he continued to call many more days after that, but I never once picked up. He left long rambling messages, never once mentioning the one thing I was most curious about: the reason for his dysfunction. I imagined the possibilities. Maybe he stuck it in a Coke bottle once and broke it. Maybe he tried to pull it off in a fit of anger one day. Maybe he had sex with too many prostitutes or masturbated too forcefully. Maybe he was just gay. In the end, none of it mattered anyway. He didn't matter, and I mattered even less.

Chapter 37

AS TIME WENT on, it became more and more difficult to move. I found myself reverting back to the way I was right after I found out about the pastor's death. I would make it to school on occasion, but I would go dressed in ripped T-shirts and baggy pants, clothes I normally wore in the house. I saw that my classmates and teachers noticed my transformation, but nobody dared say anything. I had lost all interest in school, and my marks showed it. I felt obligated to keep going since the pastor had paid the fees. The rent for my apartment had also been paid up until the end of the school year. I didn't know what I would do. It was impossible to make any sort of plans in my state.

After each lackluster day at school, I would drag myself back to my apartment and eat processed and preserved foods. I no longer had the desire to cook even the simplest of meals. Soup became my staple. Sometimes I would eat it straight from the can.

Once the school year was done, I spent my days in bed, getting up only to pee or to slurp down some soup.

When the rent was due, the landlord arrived.

"Miss Jones…Miss Jones, are you in there?" He spoke urgently as he slapped the door with his open palm.

Philomena (Unloved)

The gravitational pull had returned with a vengeance.

"Miss Jones, I know you're in there. The neighbors said you haven't left in days."

I didn't move. The next thing I heard was the sound of the door being unlocked. I had forgotten that he had the key. I pulled the cover up over my head as I waited for him to find me. It didn't take long.

"Miss Jones, I'm here for the rent. It was covered until the beginning of the month two weeks ago."

I buried myself even farther under the blanket.

I heard him walking through the apartment picking up the empty soup cans I had thrown any which way. I knew the place smelled horrible, but by then I had grown accustomed to it.

"Are you decent, Miss Jones? I'm going to open the door now."

I closed my eyes, hoping that he wouldn't see me.

"Your rent is due, Miss Jones," he repeated from the foot of my bed.

I remained completely still.

"Did you hear me, Miss Jones?"

I held my breath.

"Well, Miss Jones, I'll give you one more week to pay and then, I'm sorry, you'll have to leave."

He left and locked the door behind him.

I exhaled and wondered how I was going to get the four hundred dollars for the rent. The more I thought about it, the farther away I got from a solution. I didn't have a job. I couldn't borrow it from anyone since I didn't have any friends. I was too afraid of stealing. Disaster pending, the next week I didn't deviate from my soup-and-bed routine. I didn't see any reason to.

"So, you don't have any money at all?" the landlord asked at the end of the week.

I shook my head.

"Do you have somewhere else to go?"

I shook my head again.

"Well, I'm sorry, but you can't stay here anymore. I need tenants who can pay."

"Okay," I heard myself say, without the slightest bit of alarm or concern.

I grabbed my suitcase and began indiscriminately stuffing it. When it was filled to the brim, I sat on it and pulled the zipper shut just like I had seen Ratina do on a few occasions. Once closed, I picked it up, walked past the landlord and out the door.

"Will you be coming back for the rest of your things?" he yelled after me.

What for? I thought to myself and continued on my way.

I walked—not knowing where to go or what to do. My thoughts were completely blank. By nightfall, even though my feet ached and I was both hungry and tired, I continued to wander. I ended up dragging myself and the suitcase through the streets for exactly thirty-six hours. Completely exhausted, I found a secluded spot in a park I had once visited with Lionel. There, I lay down on the bench and fell asleep.

When I woke the next day, my suitcase was gone. The relief of not having to lug it around helped offset the distress. Being suddenly unencumbered suited me. I walked around swinging my empty arms as if I didn't have a care in the world. Just when I was beginning to feel faint from the lack of food, I saw a church. The signed outside read: *Free Meals for Everyone.* There was already a long line of people waiting. When I joined them, I didn't think of Ratina's poor opinion of beggars or how she would admonish me for taking part in such an act. All I thought about was my hunger.

Inside, as I ate the unsavory food, I examined the characters that surrounded me. I had no idea just how well I blended in. My matted hair, crumpled clothes, and frowsy stench were no different from the crowd, even though only days earlier I had had somewhere to live.

Right then, I became a member of the vagrant community: drifting like them during the day and sleeping under bridges at night. As I lay on beddings made from cardboard and newspapers, the phrase *Oh how the mighty have fallen* never once entered my mind. The same was true for the pastor, Lionel, my past, present, or future. Instead, I looked up at the shifting clouds and thought of nothing and nobody. This is what worked best.

On the streets, I was free and did as I pleased. I didn't own, or owe anyone, anything. The only schedule I had to abide was that of the church and drop-in centres where I took my meals. I roamed and lounged as I saw fit. When I felt like it, I read articles from old newspapers. It didn't matter if the stories were incomplete or dated. Sometimes when it was quiet, I spoke to myself or sang songs from my childhood. Mostly, however, I just listened to the sound of my heartbeat or the traffic or people in the distance. The muted sounds were all I needed to keep me company.

What I hated most off all was how I smelled. I knew I wasn't the only person aware of it. Sometimes people would say things like, "Get the fuck out of here, lady. You fucking stink." I knew I stank. Nobody had to tell me that. I would see people grimace or hold their nose when I got too close. I was shitting anywhere I could find cover, without the luxury of toilet paper. I also wasn't bathing properly. The sinks in the coffee shops or train station didn't suffice. The dirt was never fully removed. The residual shit in between my butt cheeks made me itch. There was no getting around it. They had showers at the shelters, but I had no change of clothes or money to wash the ones I had.

When I hadn't eaten properly, or sometimes even when I had, my mood worsened and the voices returned. I did my best to ignore them. The state of flux that I lived in didn't help. Some days I felt a bit more upbeat; other times I wished I was never born. Random vagrants, most of whose names I never bothered to learn, would comment on my fluctuating temperament. They would say, "You looking sun shiny today, Missy." Or, "Who's the grouchy bitch today? It looks like someone had a bad night under the bridge."

I wasn't proud of my new status. Who would be? I knew Ratina wouldn't have approved. If she were still alive, she would have said, "You have no pride? Didn't I teach you better than that? You're living worse than a dog or a rat in the gutter. We didn't have much, but we were always clean. It doesn't take money to be proper, just some soap and water. Look at you living like a vagabond. You want to kill me, child? You want to kill me dead?"

I didn't think it was possible, but I endured the streets for months, and then time slowly dragged out into years. The prime of my life, the time when one usually falls in love, gets married, and starts a family, was spent lying on concrete with nothing but time on my hands. I was like a fly trapped between two windows. Had I been right in my mind, I would have been able to lift myself out of the stupor, find work and another apartment, but all practical reasoning had left me. I operated only on my animal instincts. When it rained, I found shelter. When it got too cold, I found anywhere that was accessible and warm to rest my head. As I roamed the streets with plastic bags filled with junk, I felt like a prehistoric nomad going from place to place in search of food and shelter. Time was immaterial. It stood still, moved backward and sideways in a circle. The only day that I thought about changing my circumstances was the day I woke up and decided that I was going to jump.

Chapter 38

THAT MORNING UNDER the bridge, I woke chilled to the bone. I was in the habit of getting up early since that's what people do when they live in public places.

I folded up my blankets of newspapers and walked toward the shelter to get whatever they were giving out that morning.

Halfway to the shelter, it felt like someone was touching me on the shoulder. I stopped and looked around. There was no one there.

It's time, a familiar voice said.

I knew exactly what it was talking about. There was no need to ask.

I turned right around and starting walking back toward the top of the bridge where the trains crossed.

That's it, Philomena. You got it. Just close your eyes and do it. Pretend it's the ocean.

I ignored the voice because I had never learned to swim. When I looked down, there was no one in sight, so I stepped closer to the edge.

That's right, little Philomena, you can do it. No need to worry. Everything will be better after.

The voice was calmer than usual. Its tone gave me the reassurance I needed. I placed my junk on the ground, took off my shoes, and then bent over like I'd seen divers do. Then I jumped.

As I flew through the sky, I felt as light as air. I saw the ocean and lush vegetation of my home below me. Ratina and the pastor stood in the water waiting for me. There was another young man standing with them. I assumed it was my dead father who had drowned in the sea. They all looked happy as they anticipated my arrival.

I landed on my head. There was no Ratina or pastor or dead father, just concrete. There was not even any sound—just blood, lots of it. I wanted to close my eyes and not see the blood, but something kept them open. I watched as it pooled around my head. When I turned around, I saw a pair of high-heeled shoes running toward me.

"Oh my God, you're bleeding. Someone call an ambulance," she screamed.

Her voice sounded like it was coming from inside a bottle.

The blood was more black than red and didn't look like it belonged to me. I watched as frantic legs rushed silently around me, then I lost consciousness.

When I woke up in the hospital, I felt as if I had been sleeping for years.

The first person I saw was a chubby nurse with a pleasant face.

"You're in the Central Hospital," she said, seeing that I was confused.

"Why am I here? What happened?"

"The doctor will discuss that with you when he comes," she answered, then proceeded to take my temperature and my blood pressure.

"How long have I been here?"

"Almost a week."

"A week?" That didn't make any sense.

Philomena *(Unloved)*

"You've been in and out of consciousness."

"How come I don't remember waking up before?"

"I don't know. Maybe it's something to do with your fall. You'll have to ask the doctor. I'll call his office and let him know you're awake."

"Why does he have to know?"

"Because he's going to want to talk to you. All right?"

I was about to ask more questions, but she was gone before I could open my mouth.

Chapter 39

RATINA HAD THIS way about her. She would say "Thank you, Jesus" for any and every little thing. When she woke in the morning there was a *Thank you, Jesus*. When it rained, *Thank you, Jesus*. When she finished eating, *Thank you, Jesus*. Even when she passed gas there was always a *Thank you, Jesus*. The more powerful the gas, the more emphatic the *Thank you, Jesus* would be. Needless to say, she was a grateful woman. Although she had little to be grateful for. Her children had all given her their children to raise. Those children, in turn, when they were grown, followed their parents to foreign countries, never once looking back. I always told Ratina that if I ever moved away, I would make sure to send her money so that she could rest her weary bones, but she died before I could fulfil the promise.

A great source of worry for Ratina was my relationship with the pastor. Even after she had conceded that I was old enough to have a consensual relationship, she still continued to express her disapproval. She did this with her weekly firestorm of words, usually early in the morning when I was barely awake.

"That man doesn't love, you know. He will never love you. You are just more wanton flesh for him, and when he's done

Philomena (Unloved)

with you, he's going toss you aside just like he did with all of those before and after you. Thank you, Jesus."

The statement was punctuated by a burp or a fart or both.

"He is no different from any other man. They all have their urges, and they satisfy them however they see fit, even if it's with girls young enough to be their grandchild. I think the pastor even has a blasted grandchild your age! And his wife, that poor woman, to have to put up with that man all those years. God will have to give her a special corner in the sky for that. She must be some sort of saint to be able to put up with all those outside children. That man never knows when to stop. He is as old as Moses, and he's still up to the same nastiness he started back when he was young. Did I ever tell you about how he once tried to talk sweet to me when I was your age?"

My silence was the only encouragement she needed to continue.

"I was going up Old Road one day and he comes along in the opposite direction and asks me if I minded if he walked with me. We were in the same class so we knew each other well. I told him that I didn't need him to walk me anywhere and that he'd better go home to his mother. He gave me this coy smile and said, 'Good afternoon,' as if I hadn't insulted him, but then he turned around and started walking with me anyway. I stopped and told him again to go home to his mother, and you know what that fresh boy did? He tried to kiss me. I pushed him away, and he never tried anything like that with me again. That's the type of man who calls himself a man of God. I don't know what kind of God he represents. I was so vexed when the police refused to charge him with anything after we caught him with you—and then he got you pregnant! You don't know how badly I wanted to curse him out and call him all types of names. But people are not supposed speak like that to so-called holy people, but things have to be said, and he has to be called what he is—a dirty pig. The thought of you willingly lying with him turns my stomach.

You hear me? I can't take it. I have been responsible for you ever since your mother left. I know this has not been the best place for a child to be raised, but I did my best with you—you have to believe this. I did my very best with what I had. If I failed you, I am sincerely sorry. But you will not be in any better hands with that man. When I'm dead and gone, that man is not going to look after you. Yes, he'll give you small things here and there, but you will have to learn to find your own way. You understand me, Philomena?"

I nodded my head even though I wasn't in complete agreement.

"Philomena, I'm telling you this for your own good. I am not saying this to exercise my mouth. I'm telling you this because I'm not going to be here much longer, and when I'm gone you will be all alone. I don't want you to rely on that man. Finish your school and get yourself a good job. I know how bright you are. Bright girls like you can look after themselves. They don't need scallywags to look after them. Do you understand what I'm telling you, Philomena?"

I nodded.

"Good, that's a good girl. You should listen to your old grandmother. I've been here longer than you so I should know better. You still have a lot to learn and many mistakes to make."

I nodded again, hoping that she would let me sleep in peace. I told myself that I knew better than her since I had gone farther in school. I convinced myself that she was talking her usual nonsense. Wanting to put an end to her barrage I said, "Yes Ratina, I know you're right. I should leave him."

"Of course I'm right," she answered smugly.

"I know you only want the best for me."

"Of course, I do," she replied with a softness I was unaccustomed to. "Thank you, Jesus," she concluded.

Had I had any sense, I would have listened to the warnings of the old woman. She was wiser than I would ever be.

Chapter 40

I WAS CONCERNED about Cindy. I hadn't seen her the whole week following the visit with her daughter, so I went looking for her.

"I'm fine, Philomena," she said as the door to the attic swung open. She looked unusually pasty and unkempt. The odor that wafted from her room was not pleasant.

"I just haven't felt like seeing anyone is all," she began, without my asking anything. "Seeing Cher was a big kick in the gut."

I nodded my understanding.

"You want me to make you some porridge?" I offered, trying to lure her out of the room.

"Porridge? I thought they didn't eat that on your island?"

"I lied. We eat lots of it. Would you like me to make you some?"

"Sure, yeah, yeah, just let me wrap up my hair. I'll meet you downstairs."

When she arrived in the kitchen, she greeted me with a smile. I could tell that she was forcing herself to think of other things to brighten her mood. The multi-colored scarf was evidence of this.

Christene A. Browne

"I hope you put lots of sugar in it."

"I did."

"Great. That's great."

As she sat there shoveling the porridge down her throat, she didn't appear at all like the heartbroken Cindy from ten minutes before. Getting out of the room had done her some good.

Not wanting to prod or upset her, I just let her eat in peace while I kept her company.

"If Cher was your daughter, what would you do, Philomena?" Cindy asked, playing with her spoon.

"I don't know," I replied. "I don't know what it's like to be a mother."

"It's not easy being a mother, especially if you have nothing to give your kid. That's why I did what I did. I was in no shape to be anyone's mother. No one deserved to have me as a mother. I was too much like my own mother. I wanted my child to have better than me. I wanted her to have nice things, you know, like a fridge full of food and ballet lessons and all that shit. The stuff my mother couldn't give me. You know what I mean, Philomena? I was just trying to do the best for her, and look what I did instead. I messed it all up. I fucked it all up." Cindy began to cry. "Why do I have to screw everything up?"

I got up and put my hand on Cindy's shoulder and kept it there as she continued to sob.

For the next few days, I repeated the offer of the porridge, and each time she came down, she looked more and more like the old Cindy. On the fourth day, she arrived in the kitchen before me and made the cereal herself.

"Your porridge is too watery," she teased as she stood at the stove stirring the pot. "Get some bowls. I made plenty."

I obeyed and got the bowls. As we sat and ate, nothing more was said about her daughter.

Philomena (Unloved)

The following Sunday was brighter than normal. Even Susan, who rarely paid attention to the weather, took notice.

"My God, what a gorgeous day!" she exclaimed from her bed. "It's so nice, I think I just might get out there," she added without budging.

"You want to go to a barbecue with me?" Cindy asked, barging into the room. She was back to her regular attire.

"I know you're not speaking to me," Susan said, lighting a cigarette.

"No, Susan Peters, I know better than to ask you. How about it, Philomena? Look how nice it is out there. Perfect day for a barbecue."

"Yeah, Philomena, go and enjoy yourself for a change. I don't like looking at your ugly long face all the time."

"You should talk," Cindy snapped, coming to my defense.

"Do we have to take a bus?" I didn't feel like wasting the little money I had on transit.

"No, we can walk. It's in the neighborhood."

"Can I go dressed like this?" I asked, pointing at the crumpled gray sweat suit I had been wearing for days.

"Just maybe dab on some deodorant," Cindy suggested politely.

"Okay," I said as I slid out of bed and went in search of the deodorant. I agreed to go out of my concern for Cindy. I knew that appearances weren't always what they seemed.

Blinding sunshine greeted us as we stepped out the front door. Neither of us thought of turning back for shades or a hat, we just continued on.

"The woman that lives in this house reminds me of you, Philomena," Cindy said as we walked by a red brick house a few blocks from home. Susan had told me the same thing more than once. I had seen the women in passing many times, but I'd never noticed anything special about her.

"You two have the same walk, and there is something in her face, too."

I hadn't seen any of those similarities.

"Did you ever ask her where she was from?" I asked. I had my own theories. I didn't know any Africans personally, but I imagined she was from that part of the world.

"I asked her once and she just said somewhere very small," Cindy replied. "She's been living there a long time. She seems nice enough."

I nodded, and we walked on.

The house where the barbecue was taking place turned out to be farther away than Cindy had promised. It looked lopsided on the outside. In fact, many of the houses on this street were crooked. Some people said it was because of termites. Others said it was because they were built on swamp land. In any case, I imagined things rolling down the uneven floors and food falling off plates inside.

"Come on, Philomena, this way." Cindy gestured for me to follow her toward the loud music and voices in the backyard.

I froze when I saw the crowd. It had been a very long time since I had seen so many Black people amassed in one place. It reminded me of a Sunday afternoon after church back home. Only the accents were different. The people here sounded as if they were mostly Jamaicans. This was no surprise since it was Cindy's crowd.

"Cindy, gal. Where you been?" A large burly man hugged Cindy and led her away.

Left alone, I suddenly felt like a fish out of water. I wanted to run into the house, but I was too shy, so I just stood there hoping that no one would notice me. I felt bad because of how I was dressed and also since we hadn't brought anything.

Philomena *(Unloved)*

Ratina had always told me it was rude to visit a person's house empty-handed.

A slender woman grimaced at me as she approached.

"Can I offer you something to drink?" she asked in a Bajan accent. I wasn't sure if she was the host or just a friendly guest.

"No thanks," I replied. "I'm okay so far." I didn't want to have to use the bathroom.

"Okay, well, help yourself when you're ready. The drinks are inside and everything else is over there." She pointed to a long table with a large spread of food covered up with aluminum foil.

"Thanks," I said, wishing to be left alone.

I watched across the yard as Cindy chatted boisterously with a chubby man while she drank from a plastic cup. She was in her element. She noticed me, pointed to her cup, and mouthed the words, "You want some?" I shook my head, and she turned back to her conversation.

Although I felt ill at ease, there was something comforting about the gathering. I didn't feel the need to reach out and communicate with any of the strangers. I was just happy to watch them as if they were a show on TV. I grabbed an empty lawn chair, pulled it to the side away from everyone, and sat back and observed.

"Hey, there you are," the man with Cindy said, greeting a new arrival. "Come, come," he added.

Cindy took the opportunity to pour herself another drink. She motioned to me again, but I refused.

I watched as the new arrival walked by me holding the hand of a little girl who looked to be about five years old. The profile of the man looked oddly familiar.

"Lionel, so good to see you man. And who do you have there?"

"This is my daughter, Sula. Say hello to Uncle Tony, Sula."

My body stiffened. I knew that voice.

The little girl stuck her finger in her mouth and said nothing.

More than a decade had passed since I'd last seen him, but I was certain it was Lionel Thomas. He sounded happier. *The little girl must be the reason for that*, I thought. Not wanting to be seen, I got up and tried to move as inconspicuously as I could toward the front of the house.

"Philomena, where are you going?" Cindy slurred in the loudest and most annoying voice. The effects of the drinks were kicking in.

I think you should slow down. And since when do you drink? I wanted to yell back.

"Come and have a drink with me nah, man," Cindy yelled.

When I turned my head, Lionel looked straight at me. I could tell that he was trying to place me. The more he searched, the more puzzled he became.

"Philomena?" he asked. "Is that you?"

I didn't look as I had all those years ago. I had lost lots of weight, and the medications and life on the streets had aged me.

"Is it you?" Lionel let go of his daughter's hand and stepped closer. The little girl ran right behind him with her hand still in her mouth.

"Aww, they know each other." Cindy burped and took another swig of her drink.

It wasn't until Lionel was within inches of me that he was convinced.

My discomfort grew as I imagined the eyes of the whole crowd on us. I held up my hand to shield my face so that Lionel couldn't see what had become of me.

"How are you, Philomena?"

"I'm here. How about you? Your daughter?" I asked, gesturing toward the child. I was not prepared to answer any questions about all that had transpired since we last saw each other.

"Yes, this is Sula," Lionel said almost dismissively. "You've

Philomena (Unloved)

changed so much, Philomena." The tone of his voice showed his concern.

"You haven't changed at all," I replied, "except for the little one there." I didn't want to say anything more out of fear of embarrassment.

"Do you have any…any children?" Lionel asked, knowing the answer to the question.

"No, no kids," I said, looking nervously around me as if I had misplaced my imaginary children somewhere.

"Well, this is my eldest; I have two others back at home—twins," Lionel began.

While he spoke, I heard nothing but the buzz of the crowd behind us. I nodded politely to make him believe that I was taking in all that he was saying. The longer he spoke, the lighter I started to feel. I felt like a balloon being held by a child. One false move, a bump or slip, and I would have floated off into the sky. I gripped the ground firmly with my feet to prevent this from happening.

"Well, it was lovely to see you after all this time," Lionel concluded.

I could see that he wanted to offer me a hug or even a handshake, but my unsettled demeanor prevented this.

"I'm going to go and look for something to eat and drink for this one," he said, pointing to his daughter with his chin. "Nice to see you again."

Cindy came to join me the minute Lionel was gone.

"Nice, Philomena. Nice on you. Your old boyfriend that?" she asked.

I could smell the alcohol on her breath.

"So, you weren't a nun after all."

"Can we go now?"

"We just got here. And you haven't had anything to eat or drink yet. Come, let's get some curry goat and rice. Marcia makes the best goat."

"No, thank you. I'm going to go. You can stay, but I'm going to go."

I turned around and walked to the front of the house. The light-headedness that I'd experienced while Lionel spoke returned the moment I got back onto the sidewalk. One look at the crooked house made me nauseous. Wanting to get away from it and Lionel as quickly as I could, I starting jogging. My heart was beating out of my chest. After only a few minutes, I was forced to stop to catch my breath. I wasn't accustomed to exerting myself. I took some deep breaths to stop my head from spinning. After checking to make sure no one was following me, I continued the rest of the way at a slower pace. The voices came when I was a safe distance away.

You should have stayed at the party you dumb fuck. No one was going to do anything to you there. They were just trying to be friendly.

What the fuck are you talking about? They would have killed her if she'd stayed. They would have stabbed her in the back with one of those plastic knives. Didn't you see how many of those knives there were on the table? They were all just waiting for her to get close enough to them so they could do her in. All they really needed to get was two clean jabs of her eyes—poke them right out and then watch her bleed to death. That would have been their entertainment for the night. Those evil bastards.

You fucking idiot. The only bastard there was you—nobody else. You stupid fucking bitch. You're the stupid fucking bitch falling for a man who was just using you and letting go a man who was so much better.

Where the fuck are you going now? Do you even know the way home? Don't go and get fucking lost now.

He's dead.

Philomena (*Unloved*)

Who the fuck are you talking about now?

Him.

Of course he's dead. When people die, they're dead. No more. Nothing. Gone. Good-bye.

I didn't even get to say good-bye. He was so far away when he died.

That's ancient history. Why are you rehashing ancient history? Nobody cares about that shit. He didn't care about you.

Yes, he did. He cared about me.

Then why did he let you go? Why did he die on you like that without telling you in advance, without any warning letter or anything?

How was he supposed to do that?

Are you sure you're going the right way?

Did you make a wrong turn? Isn't the house the other way?

He didn't love anyone, especially not you. He just used you.

He just used you.

He just used you up and spit you out.

He's dead and there is not a fucking thing you can do about it.

You killed him. You made him die. You're responsible. You shouldn't have left him. You should have stayed by his side forever. You killed him. You fucking bitch, you killed him.

The voices raged on as I got closer to the red brick house. They stopped abruptly when I got within a few feet of it. The older woman was there walking up the stairs. I couldn't see her face, but there was something in her movement that seemed familiar for the very first time. Maybe Cindy's and Susan's observations weren't that farfetched. The way the woman swayed her shoulders with a slight twist reminded me of Ratina. I made an attempt to see her face again, even though I had seen it a million times before, but the door slammed shut before I could. A sense of calm washed over me as I walked on.

Chapter 41

WHEN I ARRIVED at the rooming house, I noticed Janice sitting on the porch. This was a rare sight since I hardly ever saw her outside. She looked troubled. A silk scarf around her neck only added to the strangeness. In all the years I'd known her, I had never seen her wear any type of scarf before. I wondered if she'd finally caught on about her neck.

"Hi, Philomena, where are you getting back from?" she asked.

I gave her a look. She had never asked me any such question before. She wasn't in the habit of asking much. She normally kept to herself in her office.

"A barbecue with Cindy," I answered.

"What happened to her?" Janice asked, almost in panic as if outings with me always led to disaster.

"I left her there," I said as I opened the front door.

"Why did you leave her there?"

"She was drinking and…"

"Drinking! Did you say she was drinking?"

"Yes," I said, wondering what was so unusual about that.

"She hasn't…she's been sober since she's been here." Janice was now on her feet.

"Do you know what started her off? Do you know what happened to make her start again? She was doing so well all this time."

"I didn't know she had a problem."

"Yes, she did, she does. Do you know what happened? What made her…?"

I was starting to think that I was bad luck. Ratina once told me that she knew how to put spells on people. Maybe she had put a spell on me to curse anyone I got close to.

"She went to see her daughter."

"Her daughter? When did that happen?"

"A few weeks ago."

"I didn't know that she was allowed to see her."

"The daughter lives with her mother now."

"Cindy's mother?" Janice seemed even more alarmed.

"Yes."

"Maybe we should go and get her to a meeting right away. You think we should do that?" Janice seemed so uncertain. From the sounds of it, I don't think she had ever been involved in any kind of intervention before. This was strange given her line of work.

"Could you take me to where she is?"

I shook my head emphatically. "I can't go back there."

"But we have to stop her from drinking and get her to a meeting. What street was it on?"

I realized that I hadn't taken note of the street name. I had just followed along blindly.

"I think it's the one right after Elm St."

"You mean Oak?"

"No, the one with all those crooked houses."

"You mean Pine?"

"Yeah, I think that's it."

"Which house? Look, Philomena, why don't you just come with me. It'll make things a lot easier."

Philomena (Unloved)

"I can't. I'm sorry. You'll have to go on your own. It was a blue house. All you have to do is go to the one with all the noise and people. It wouldn't be hard to find."

"Can you watch things here for me while I'm gone?"

I nodded, not sure of what there was to watch.

Janice ran into the house in front of me, grabbed the pouch she kept her car keys in, and ran right back out like it was a matter of life and death.

❧

The house was quiet, as usual. There was no one in the TV room or the kitchen. Susan was sleeping when I got upstairs. I lay down on my bed to rest my eyes, hoping that the voices would leave me alone.

Thirty minutes later I heard some commotion downstairs. Janice had returned.

"Can someone give me a hand, please!" she yelled from the bottom of the stairs.

I pulled myself out of bed and went down.

Cindy was in terrible shape. She looked as if she had been to war and back. She was resting her full weight on Janice.

"I need you to help me get her up to her room. I got her to drink some coffee, and her sponsor will be here first thing in the morning to take her to a meeting. He said it would probably be best to just let her sleep it off tonight and keep a close eye on her. Can you grab her other arm?"

Cindy's arm was as limp as a piece of overcooked spaghetti, but a hundred times heavier. It was a struggle getting her up the stairs. Both Janice and I were sweating buckets by the time we got her into bed.

Cindy hadn't said a word the whole time. She barely opened her eyes.

While Janice tucked her into bed, I realized that I had never once set foot in Cindy's room. The room was tidier than what I had expected and a true reflection of her. It was plastered with the colors of the Jamaican flag, and all sorts of Caribbean knickknacks were placed throughout. Cher's blue dog sat next to her baby picture.

As Cindy drifted off, Janice, with the precision of a prison guard, checked under the bed, in the closet, and in the drawer to make sure there was no alcohol stashed away.

"Do you still need me?" I asked.

"Yeah, could you just go downstairs and bring some water. She may get thirsty in the middle of the night."

"Sure," I said and left.

I had never seen Janice so caring. She had kept that side of her hidden so well for so many years.

Susan was conveniently wide awake and nosing around Cindy's room when I returned with the water.

"What's the water for?" Susan asked.

"It's in case she gets up in the middle of the night."

"That woman is dead to the world. An atomic bomb couldn't wake her."

Susan was right. Cindy was out cold.

Chapter 42

I DIDN'T SEE Cindy again until three days later when she appeared ghost-like in the kitchen. I had just grabbed the sugar from the cupboard, and there she was. I didn't even hear when she came in. I could tell that she had seen her doctor and had been given some strong medication.

"How are you doing there, Cindy?" I asked, even though I could see that she was far from good.

"I'm all right. Hanging in there," she replied, not sounding at all like herself. "You're making tea?"

"Yes, do you want some?"

"Yeah, why not. The coffee is all gone, right?"

"Yeah," I replied as I retrieved a second mug from the cupboard.

Cindy sat down at the table and clasped her hands together.

"My doctor said that it would probably be a good idea if I didn't see my daughter again for a while. He said I needed to give her some time."

"That makes sense."

"The messed-up thing is that she's with my mother. Who told them that was going to be good for her?"

"They must know what they're doing."

"They never know what they doing, Philomena. They just pretend that they do. My mother used to beat the hell out of me. One time she even did it in front of one of my friends. I was twelve years old and we wanted to go swimming, but my swimsuit was wet because I had used it the day before. I only had the one. So I put it on and put my clothes on over it. I don't know who told me to do that. On the way out the door, she stops me and my friend and starts interrogating me. 'Why is your shirt wet, Cindy?' 'It's not wet,' I said. 'Yes, it is,' she yelled. 'You don't think I have two eyes in my head to see? You think I'm stupid, blind, deaf, or dumb?' She was always asking us that. One time I said 'yes' and she whipped me good. She knew something wasn't right with my shirt, so she came close to me and felt it and saw that I had my bathing suit on. You would have thought I'd stolen money from the Pope or something. She said, 'Where the hell do you think you're going with that wet bathing suit? Are you retarded or something?' She was always asking us that, too. I swear, with the amount of licks she gave us in the head, she could have given us all brain damage. For the wet bathing suit, she didn't hit me in the head though. She just grabbed a shoe and beat me on my arms and back. I was lucky she didn't get her hands on the extension cord. My friend was smart enough to get the hell out of there. When I saw her later, I just laughed the whole thing off as if it didn't matter.

"You know the only person who I could talk to about my mother was Trevor Number Two. His mother use to beat him too. That was actually our first conversation, arguing about who got worse licks. He won though. He showed me a mark on his head where his mother had burnt him with an iron. My mother never left anything permanent like that. Cuts, welts, scrapes, and all that—nothing that would send any of us to the hospital though. Sorry for rambling on like this, Philomena. The doctor got me going. He asked me all these questions and I played

Philomena *(Unloved)*

dumb like I didn't know what he was talking about. And now listen to me! I'm talking about all the things he asked me about. Tough shit for him. How am I supposed to talk with someone who has this fucked up look on his face all the time like he has to take a shit or something? I always want to ask the fucker, 'You need a break to go to the bathroom or something? I could wait, you know.' But I just watch his stupid face and think about what I'm going to do with the rest of my day. He always ends each session by saying, 'I think we made some good progress today, Cynthia.' I hate when the fucker calls me that. Why can't he call me Cindy like everyone else? And the fucking progress that he's talking about is all in his fucking head. We're not making any progress. We're not doing anything there but wasting my time and his. I'm sure he's just relieved that he can take his shit once our hour is up."

Cindy was now looking more alive. I guess all she needed was to unload some of the things she had been carrying around with her.

"What was your mother like, Philomena? I never heard you talk about her. I never really heard you talk about anyone for that matter. You're real quiet. Trevor Number One was like that. He had to be in a real special mood to talk."

"I didn't grow up with my mother."

"Yeah, that's common. Who raised you, your grandmother?"

"Yeah."

"Did she beat you?"

"Sometimes."

"What happened to your mother?"

"She's supposed to be somewhere up here."

"Have you looked for her?"

I nodded. I didn't feel like speaking about my mother.

"Mothers are a piece of work, aren't they?"

I gave a silent nod.

Chapter 43

DOCTOR RUEBEN CAME the next day, just as the nurse had promised. He spoke to me in a calm manner, but to my ears, it sounded otherwise. The wound on my head was causing me a great amount of pain.

"Nice to see you up, Mrs. Jones. We were worried about you for a bit when you were in the coma," he began.

"Could you speak a little softer please?" I asked, holding my head. The bandages had just been changed.

"I thought I was speaking softly," the doctor said.

"It sounds like you're yelling."

"But I'm not yelling at all. I assure you, I'm speaking in my normal voice."

"But it still sounds like yelling."

"But, I'm not yelling or speaking loudly. I promise you. I know—"

"You call that not yelling?" I snapped. His voice sounded like a jackhammer pounding my head. I just wanted him to stop.

"I can see that you are in a bit of distress there, Mrs. Jones. It's to be expected." He took a few steps toward me. The hard soles of his shoes screeched across the floor.

Philomena (*Unloved*)

"Why is everything so fucking loud?" I yelled as I continue to pull at my bandage. The nurse had put it on too tight.

"Please, Mrs. Jones. You really shouldn't be touching that."

"It's too tight, and you're still speaking too loud."

"Mrs. Jones—please."

"Mrs. Jones! I'm not married so could you please fucking stop calling me that!" I heard myself say. It was very unlike me to curse. Ratina would have tanned my hide for that.

"Such language is not at all necessary, Miss Jones," the doctor said, grabbing hold of my hand.

I repelled his hand and screamed, "Don't touch me. Don't fucking touch me. Don't you ever fucking touch me."

The doctor recoiled. I could tell that I frightened him. I was frightening myself.

"Please calm down, Mrs., I mean Miss, Jones. It's not good to get so worked up in your condition."

"Calm down! I'm not fucking calming down. I just don't want you to fucking touch me. You hear me? I don't want anybody fucking touching me anymore."

When he took a cautious step toward me, I began flailing my arms and screaming.

"Stay away from me. Stay the fuck away from me. I don't want your grubby hands all over me. Don't you ever fucking touch me again!"

I watched as he eased over to the wall and pressed the yellow in-case-of-emergency button.

"Rape! Rape!" I yelled. I had never uttered that word before.

Two nurses came running in.

"Rape! Rape!" I continued.

"We need to calm her down," the doctor said.

"I'm fucking calm. I told you!" I said, screaming at the top of my lungs. I don't think I had screamed that loud in my whole life. My head was really throbbing.

One nurse, the larger of the two, came closer to me while the other flew out of the room.

"Don't come near me. Don't fucking touch me. I don't want anyone touching me!" I said to the one nurse who was struggling with my flapping arms. I did everything in my power to keep her from restraining me. In the process, I hit her in the face. I wasn't sure if it was on purpose or by accident. The harder she tried to pin down my arms, the more aggressive I became.

"Don't fucking touch me," I said. "Nobody gave you permission to touch me."

"I'm just trying to help you, dear," the nurse said as calmly as she could.

"I don't need your fucking help!" I yelled back.

"They're going to lock you up if you don't stop," the nurse said under her breath as she continued to battle with me.

"We don't lock people up here, Nurse Davis," the doctor corrected. He was now watching all the commotion from a safe distance. "We place them in a safe environment where they are not a danger to themselves or to anyone else."

The nurse grimaced as she continued to try to confine me.

The second nurse returned with two large orderlies. I wasn't intimidated by them. I kept swinging my arms and fighting no matter how much my head hurt. I was determined to not let them get me. I had been touched enough. Miss Pierce had touched me with her large manly hands, large lopsided breasts, and her foul-smelling privates. I didn't want any more of it. I didn't want to be touched by her or anyone else, ever again. The only person in the world who I would have consented to touch me at the moment was dead. But there was a time when I would have given my life for him to stop touching and torturing me. There was a time when I felt like I could kill him for hurting me and for doing all the perverse things that he forced me to do, like putting his slimy penis into my mouth. I wanted to gag from the musky, salty taste. So many times, I wanted to bite the thing in two and spit it in his face.

"Just grab either side of her," the second nurse ordered the two large men.

The orderlies did as they were told and moved to my side and seized my arms.

I was panting like a dog in need of water.

"What are you trying to do—break my fucking arms?" I yelled, but deep down I just wanted them to stop. I had no more fight left.

Once I gave in, or the orderlies succeeded—I'm not sure which it was—the second nurse took a needle and plunged it into my arm. The men held me tight as they waited for the drug to take effect. As I tried to lift my head in one last feeble protest, the room went black. When I woke up, I was alone and naked in a white room.

Chapter 44

HAD RATINA BEEN alive, I would have been able to ask her for my mother's address. I knew the return address on the airmail envelopes was no longer valid since she had moved many times. I couldn't ask any of her siblings because they were scattered all over the world. Thinking that my dead father's family could help, I paid them a visit shortly before I left home.

I didn't really know them since I only saw them occasionally at church or in town. Ratina told me that they gave her money to help with my upbringing whenever they felt the spirit.

"Take this little piece of thing for the child," they would say and press some bills into Ratina's palm.

"Thank you, Jesus," Ratina would always reply, even though Jesus had nothing to do with it.

Their house was ten times larger and nicer than Ratina's. The pale yellow was always freshly painted, and the verandah that went around the whole house was much fancier than the three concrete blocks that led up to Ratina's shack.

Sylvia, my dead father's mother, was sitting cooling herself on the lavish verandah when I arrived.

"Good afternoon," I said as I rested my foot on the first step. I could tell that she didn't recognize me at first.

"Good afternoon."

"How are you doing today, Grandmother?" I felt very strange calling her that. Ratina had been my one and only grandmother.

"Oh—I'm fine, child. How are you?"

"I am going to America in a few days."

"Yes, I heard."

"I wanted to ask you if you had an address for my mother."

"Your mother?" I knew she didn't care much for her.

"Yes, I wanted to contact her."

"Your mother…I don't have any idea what her address is. Why would you think I have it? Since she left…"

Ratina had told me that my mother had left on bad terms with the family both times.

"Well I thought I would just try." I retrieved my foot from the step. *What a waste of time*, I thought. "Good afternoon," I added as I turned to leave.

"Wait, child. Pansy just fried up some fish. Would you like some?"

"No, no thanks," I said and went on my way.

Ratina had told me not to upset myself too much about the negligence of my dead father's people. She told me that they had nothing against me. It was my mother who they disliked. The first time I had asked Ratina why, she said, "They just have bad minds." I had to ask several times before I got the full story.

My mother had been one of the prettiest girls in the parish, and my father one of the handsomest boys, so when they got together everyone saw a great match. His family, however, saw the opposite. My mother was a touch too poor and dark for their liking.

The complexion of my father's family had gotten progressively lighter over the generations from the descendants marrying themselves off to "whitish-looking" people, even if these people were penniless. So, when my dead father told his mother that he was in love with my mother, they did their best to dissuade him.

"Look how black and ugly she is, and every man on the island has already had her."

My father disagreed and was in love, so he married my mother anyway. From the moment my mother moved into my father's house, she was completely ignored by the rest of the family. To make up for this, my father would indulge her and give her everything she wanted.

He was always doing silly things to make her smile when he saw that she was feeling low.

The day on the beach when he drowned was such an occasion.

"Cheer up why don't you, my sweet. I don't like seeing you so glum."

"Your family…"

"Just because they're miserable doesn't mean you have to be too."

"You know we could move. You make enough money."

"That house is plenty big for all of us. Nobody bothers us up on the second floor. That's our part of the house and don't let them ever tell you any differently. This baby, and all the babies we have, will always have a home there," he said as he touched my mother's big belly.

"Okay," my mother said, conceding.

"Are you hungry?" my father asked as he jumped up and started running into the water.

"No. Where are you going?"

"I'm going to catch you some fish for dinner," he yelled back as he reached the water.

"You're so silly," my mother giggled.

"Just watch me now. I'm going to catch them with my teeth."

My mother giggled even more and watched as my father

Philomena *(Unloved)*

dove into the water. She smiled and waited for him to resurface. After a few minutes, when he hadn't reappeared, she flew into a panic and ran toward the water.

"My husband, he hasn't come back. Somebody, please help!"

A young man ran into the water after him. He plunged his head into the water, then came back up.

"I can't see anything under there, and I can't swim."

"Can anybody swim?" my mother screamed frantically. When nobody replied she knew that my father was as good as dead. His body was never recovered. They said it was most likely pulled away by an undercurrent.

What a terrible way to die, I thought.

Chapter 45

AS SUMMER GAVE way to fall, things had more or less normalized in the house. Cindy was feeling better. She had gotten the help she needed from her sponsor. The others were mourning Heike a little less each day and getting back to their regular selves—Janice to her crosswords, Susan to her stories.

One night, just as I placed my head on my pillow, Susan put out her cigarette, sat up in her bed, and looked me straight in the eye, something she rarely did.

"There was once a girl who wished she could live in a Barbie Dream House," Susan began.

I settled into my bed to listen.

"Well," Susan continued, "to surprise her one day, the girl's father brought home the biggest Barbie Dream House she had ever seen. She beamed as he placed it in front of her. It had all the fixings that she could imagine. 'What do you say?' the father prodded. 'Thank you,' she answered hesitantly. She was never quite sure what her father wanted to hear. He was easily provoked and had already thrown out all of her other toys in fits of anger.

Philomena (Unloved)

'Thank you, who?' the father said. 'Thank you, Daddy,' she said as she nervously inched closer to the toy. She wanted to be able to enjoy it before it vanished.

"As she pushed and moved the miniature furniture all about inside the house, she escaped into an imaginary world—one that she never wanted to return from, but the truth was, reality was never far away. There was the dismal living room, where all the furniture had been sold off. The girl knew it had something to do with the needles her parents stuck in their arms. They always went into the bathroom and closed the door. Sometimes they would be in there for hours and forget to feed her. When she got hungry, she made air sandwiches with two plain slices of bread. 'Can I go in there with you?' she had asked her mother one day as she was about to close the bathroom door. 'What the fuck do you want to do in there?' her mother had replied. 'It's not for kids.' 'Well it seems like fun.' 'You don't know what the fuck you're talking about. Just go and fucking play like kids are supposed to.' One of her favorite games was called Catch Me If You Can. It involved catching and killing roaches. One day she got thirty of them.

"The only bed in the apartment was in her room. The girl thought that the bed was not really just for her but for her father who visited every night once her mother was out like a light. He came in the room the first time on her fifth birthday. Her present that day was a bite on her father's 'salty wiener,' as he called it. She didn't like the taste, but her father told her that he would get her a puppy. He lied of course."

"Why are you telling such stories, Susan?" I interrupted, even though I knew the answer. Susan and I had something in common—and it was something I had never suspected.

"Because I feel like it," she replied. "The doctor said—"

"Yeah, I know what the doctor said," I replied. "Why haven't you ever told that story before? I've heard all your other stories many times, but never that one."

"I just felt like telling that one today."

"Why today of all days?"

"It just came out."

"I see," I said and left it at that.

"Can I continue now?" she asked.

"Sure, go ahead."

As I sat and listened to the rest of Susan's story, I knew only small parts of it were actually true. Susan had a great way of hiding behind her stories. They insulated her against the world. I wondered about all that had happened to her along the way to shape her into the person she was today. *Her journey must have been as perilous as mine*, I thought. The fact that we never spoke openly about it was telling.

After Susan finished her story, she looked me straight in the eye again and said, "Good night, Philomena. Sweet dreams." She rested her head down on her pillow and closed her eyes.

The story had agitated me. It was, however, a peaceful sort of agitation—if that is even possible. In hearing it, I was forced to rethink some of the things that had happened to me. In the moments after the story, I no longer felt like the little girl who had been a victim but instead like the woman who had endured and survived. Susan reminded me that I wasn't alone in my suffering. Not being able to express my gratitude properly, I said, "Good night, Susan. Sweet dreams to you too."

I got up and left the room, feeling the need for some air.

Chapter 46

THE WIND WAS very temperamental outside. As I walked down the dark street, Susan's story was still on my mind. The more I thought about it, I realized that the girl in the story had more in common with me than with Susan. Maybe Susan was trying to tell me my own story in her odd way. Except, I didn't know what a Barbie was until I came to America, my parents weren't drug addicts, and it wasn't my father who had abused me.

As I continued, I tried to put the morbid thoughts out of my head. I didn't see a soul until I walked a block and turned the corner. The door of the red brick house down the street was opening. I slowed my pace in order to get a better look at this person who everyone said reminded them of me. I wanted to see just what it was that everyone else saw. The old woman and I had exchanged quiet waves and nods for many years but had never once spoken. The apathy that I felt most days was probably the reason for this. From my observations, good neighborliness wasn't something that was widely practiced in this culture. Back home, everyone knew their neighbors and their neighbor's neighbors. The relationships may not have been close but they were friendly. I had heard stories about people living next door to someone for years in America and never exchanging words, but I didn't believe that it was possible. This lady wasn't my direct neighbor, but she was someone who I passed on a regular basis. The fact that we were both Black could have been something that facilitated a friendship, but in this case, it hadn't.

I was one house away by the time the woman reached her bottom step. I took my time as I approached to examine her face in a way I had never done before. There was something familiar about it. Something in the upper part of it reminded me of Ratina. She paused and gave me a puzzled looked. It was almost one of recognition. She smiled and waved, then she turned and started walking away in front of me. Her gait was sluggish, befitting a woman of her age. I slowed my step even more so that I wouldn't pass her. As we were continuing on our way, I started to put my mind in another place, a blank space, but then the old lady turned around abruptly.

"Where are your people from?" she asked. Her accent was oddly familiar. She didn't sound at all like someone from Africa.

"Montserrat," I replied.

She froze.

"Montserrat," she repeated, stunned.

She stepped toward me and moved her face closer to mine.

"Sorry, I can't see so good. My eyes are bad," she said as she scrutinized my face up close. "I have never met a single soul from Montserrat for as long as I've been here, and I've been here a very long time. Montserrat is where I'm from."

I stared into her eyes and nodded. The closer I looked, the more familiar they appeared.

"Which part?" she asked, moving uncomfortably close.

"St. Peter's," I replied.

"Which part of St. Peters?"

Philomena *(Unloved)*

"My grandmother's house was close to Bunkum Bay."

"Oh my goodness—Ratina! Ratina the fortune teller—is that who you belong to?"

She covered her mouth with one hand while her purse slipped out of the other.

I nodded my head.

"Then…then…that makes you Donna's daughter then," she said as she stooped down to retrieve the purse.

I nodded my head again, completely mesmerized by the fact that she knew my mother.

"You knew Donna, my mother?" I felt as light as air all of a sudden—like I was about to drift away.

"Do you know who I am?" she asked with a smirk.

I shook my head, puzzled, searching her face for clues. "Should I know you?"

"No, of course not. You wouldn't remember me. I was your mother's classmate. I left home a few years after her. You would have been too small to remember me.

"Yes, she and I were in the same class from standard one to fifth form. She was always a nice, tidy girl. We used to call her 'neaty' because she was so neat. She was very proper, and her hair and clothes always had to be just so…"

As I listened to the stranger describe my mother, a woman who was just as strange to me as the woman standing here in front of me, I did my best to try to control the spasms that were erupting in my body. Each part of me seemed to want to move independently. One part wanted to fly away and find the woman who was being described, wherever she was, dead or alive. The other part wanted to remain right there and take in all that the stranger had to share with me.

Ratina had purposely told me very little about what my mother was like as a child. She had no time or energy or desire for such indulgences.

"…she was also very smart. One of the smartest in the class," the lady continued. "I know she is supposed to be up here somewhere, but I've never seen her. I would love to see her again."

I was about to tell her all about how I searched for my mother in vain on my arrival, but I decided not to. Speaking of it wouldn't bring any resolution. I had long since given up hope of ever seeing my mother again. In my heart of hearts, I believed that she was no longer living since I wasn't able to feel her essence as I once did.

The woman stepped back and began to examine the whole of me this time. After her examination was complete, she looked back in the direction of the red brick house where she lived.

"You know, I just made some sweet potato pudding this morning." There was a hint of trepidation in her voice. "Would you like to come up to my place to taste some? I was going to pick up a few rolls of toilet paper that's on sale at the drugstore, but the sale lasts until the end of the week, so I can go another time. Would you like to come up?"

From the apprehensive look on her face, I got the impression that she was not in the habit of making such invitations.

Inwardly, I was anxious to hear more about my mother. Outwardly, I appeared indifferent as I stared blankly back at the red brick house.

"Would you like to?" she repeated, seeming less hesitant this time.

I looked at her face once again and felt an awkward smile wash over my own face. It was a smile that required no effort at all. It came from the depths of my soul and had nothing to do with the smiles that I often faked to be polite or just to display that I was still in touch with my humanity.

As I followed the woman back to the house and up the stairs, I felt a warmth radiating throughout my body. I wasn't sure where the sensation was coming from, possibly the same place that the smile had emerged from.

The tiny apartment on the first floor of the house was cluttered. Piles of newspapers and overflowing boxes were everywhere. The floor was barely visible. Junk was piled high on all the furniture. The smell was odd and unpleasant. It was as if pieces of food had been lost and left to rot. I could tell from the way she moved about as if everything were normal, she no longer noticed. I assumed that she spent most of her time in the small blue armchair, since it was one of the only spots that was easily accessible. From the pillow nearby, it appeared as if she might have slept there too. Given the overall state of the place, I could see why she had been hesitant about inviting me up.

She took some clothes off the armchair and motioned for me to sit. With little effort, she took some boxes off another chair and moved it closer to where I was seated.

"Would you like some juice or tea with the sweet potato pudding?" she asked as she uncomfortably picked at the fabric at the back of the chair.

"I don't want to put you to any trouble." I offered, wondering if she would be able to find her kettle and teapot in the jungle of mess.

"Oh, it's not any trouble at all." It appeared that she was trying to remember something. "Juice or tea?"

"Tea then, please," I said, hoping it wouldn't be too much trouble.

"Okay, I will be right back."

I listened as she banged about in the kitchen. I imagined that it was even more cluttered in there. While I waited, I searched the room for clues of her life and the odd odor. The mass of junk was too much to make sense of.

"I remember Ratina used to make the best sweet potato pudding," she began as she returned from the kitchen with two plates, each with two squares of sweet potato pudding. The hissing sound from the stove told me that she had indeed found her kettle.

Christene A. Browne

"You're okay eating with your fingers?" she asked, passing me a plate. "I think it tastes better with your fingers anyway," she continued, shoving a chunk of the sticky dessert into her mouth.

We ate in silence for a bit. The taste of the pudding brought me back to when I was a child and Ratina would make large batches of it to sell to the school children during their lunch hour. It had been my job to scrape out the pans and clean up the mess. As I wallowed in nostalgia and my memory of Ratina, the strange lady, whose name I had not yet learned, cleaned off her plate, got up from her seat, and left again. She returned this time with two mugs.

"I put a little sugar and milk in for you. Is that okay?"

"Yes, thank you." I nodded.

She examined my face once again as she handed me the mug.

"You know, I think you take more after your father."

"You knew my father too?"

"Of course, we were all in class together. Oh boy was he sweet on your mother. I think he loved her all the way from the beginning."

"The beginning?"

"From the time we started school."

"Oh."

"Those two were inseparable. He even stuck with her when she got sick, when no one else wanted anything to do with her."

I had no idea what she was talking about. I hadn't heard of any illness my mother had had before leaving home. My curiosity was piqued.

"But this was long before you were born; you wouldn't know anything about that."

"What was the matter with her?" I asked, beginning to suspect what it may have been.

"There wasn't anything wrong with her body. She was as fit as a fiddle. It was a different type of sickness, the type that

Philomena *(Unloved)*

people get when they feel too much. You know what I mean?" She pointed to her head.

I sat back in the chair for the first time. I was right, my mother and I had the same awful affliction in common. I wondered what had brought hers on, or if she had been born with a disposition for it. Maybe I had been born with the same disposition, and all that had happened to me only brought things to the surface.

"They said she had some sort of breakdown. It happened when we were in third form. She just started crying in class one day, and the more anyone tried to talk to her and console her, the worse the crying got. They sent for Ratina, and by the time she got there, your mother was out of control."

"Did anyone know what happened to her?"

"Till this day, I don't know what happened. All I know is that your father visited her every day in the hospital."

"They put her in the hospital?"

"Yeah, we didn't have a hospital for crazy people like they have here, so they put her in the regular hospital. And your father, the good person that he was, he would visit her every day and take her whatever schoolwork we'd done in class. When she got out of the hospital, nobody would go near her. It was like she had leprosy or something. But your father, he was always at her side and chastised anyone who made fun of her. He was a good person. It was a shame he died the way he did. It's a shame you never got to meet him."

I was at a loss for words. As the woman spoke, I felt a warm sensation growing inside of me. With each of her words and slight movement of her body, I was transported back in time to a place I had long forgotten. I was taken back home. Being there, listening to her accent and eating the pudding, reminded me of my history, my story, my origins. I had lived my whole life with a feeling of displacement, of not belonging to the world or anything in it. Ratina was the only person who had fully claimed me, but I wasn't her child. The two who had given me life were absent my whole life, and I knew that had had a detrimental impact on me. But with this woman's words, I felt I was somehow regaining a sense of that belonging, a part of myself that I didn't know existed or had somehow forgotten. I did belong somewhere. I had a home once. I had a family once. But now that family consisted of the women in the house. I had never thought about Susan or Cindy in that way before, no matter how much we had been through. Now they were the only family I knew. We were connected not only by our shared secrets, how we had been violated and unloved, but also by the resilience that comes from such experiences. Even though our trauma had not demonstrated to us what love truly was, we had learned to love. We loved each other in our own way. The word *love* was never used and none of us would have ever admitted to even liking the others, but there was love in that house of damaged souls. It took the stranger's stories about my dead family for me to realize that I had somehow acquired a new family.

For the next few hours, the cluttered mess around me, along with the distasteful scent, vanished as I sat without moving while this woman shared all the stories she had about my mother, my father, Ratina, and my former home. With the stories of my mother and father's relationship, I began to have a deeper appreciation and understanding of what love was and realized that it had been within me all along. It had never left. It might have been why I was still alive.

Ratina once told me that God places everything we need close at hand, we just have to open our eyes to see those things. Ratina couldn't have been more right. The women in the house—Susan, Cindy, maybe even Janice—and now this woman, who I had barely noticed before, had all been placed in my life for a purpose. As I continued listening to her, I repeated Ratina's words in my head, "Thank you, Jesus," I said. Ratina would have been so pleased.

Acknowledgments

WRITING IS A solitary act, but I could not have completed this book without the help and support of others.

I would like firstly to thank my readers, Kathy Tihane, Menbere Gabreselassie, and Brenda Roach for your honest feedback, input, and thought-provoking insights.

To my family and friends who always have my back and expect great things from me. To the beautiful souls who are my children Daley, Maya, and Jonah, thanks for your inspiration and teaching me much more than I can ever teach you.

To my grandmothers, Mother Rannie and Mary Adina, I thank you for your continual inspiration.

To Carolyn Jackson, Kathryn Cole, and Margie Wolfe at Second Story Press thanks for your continual support and for saying yes again. Thanks also to Kathryn White and the Ontario Arts Council for your contribution.

Lastly, and most of all, I would like to acknowledge and thank the anonymous stranger and all the women whom I've known who inspired me to write this book. I hope I have done your stories justice.

About

CHRISTENE BROWNE IS an award-winning filmmaker whose work has been broadcast and screened internationally. With the making of *Another Planet* in 1999, Browne became the first Black woman to direct and write a dramatic feature film in Canada. In 2011 she was awarded the Visionary award by the the WIFT Foundation for her ground-breaking documentary series, *Speaking in Tongues: The History of Language,* which features Noam Chomsky. Her first novel, *Two Women*, was published in 2013.

She is currently completing a feature length documentary and working as a lecturer in the Radio and Television Arts program at Ryerson University.